# KAVIK THE WOLF DOG

# KAVIK THE WOLF DOG

**Walt Morey**

Illustrated by Peter Parnall

AN
**APPLE**
PAPERBACK

SCHOLASTIC INC.
New York Toronto London Auckland Sydney

ISBN 0-590-44113-2

12 11 10 9 8 7 6 5 4 3 2                                    1 2 3 4 5/9

Printed in the U.S.A.                                            28

*This book is dedicated to
all young people from six to sixty
who have known the love of an animal.*

# illustrations

# *chapter 1*

CHARLIE ONE EYE LIFTED THE SQUIRMING pup by the scruff of the neck, and looked at him. His careless grip pinched the pup's tender skin, and he wriggled and whimpered in protest. But the man studied him with no concern. The whimper turned to a growl. Suddenly the pup twisted his head and sank tiny needle-sharp teeth in Charlie's thumb.

Charlie One Eye dropped the pup. His big hand struck, and with a startled yelp of pain and surprise the pup was knocked rolling. He gathered himself and charged back to the attack, growling with puppy ferocity. Again the hand sent him spinning and howling. He was up and was bowled end over end a third time. Once more he wobbled uncertainly to his feet, prepared to do battle.

The hand swept up—and the pup stopped. He had learned painfully what that hand could do. He sank to his belly in the grass, eyes on the upraised hand. The hand lifted him. He continued to growl and show his teeth. But he did not attempt to bite.

"You learn quick who's boss," Charlie One Eye said. "And you got fight. I like that."

Charlie studied the small growling bundle with his one good eye. "You've got wolf in you," he said. "You've got the shape, the feet and head and the eyes. You're gonna be big, strong, smart, and tough. Mean, too." Charlie One Eye was struck with a surprising thought.

He'd raised sled dogs to sell. Twice in the past he had tried to win the North American Sled Dog Derby at Fairbanks. A win would have made his dogs greatly sought after, and twice as valuable. But each time he'd lost because his lead dog collapsed. A good team begins with a good leader, and he'd never had one. In his mind's eye he saw this pup full grown and trained, the head of a team of strong, willing dogs. The old desire to try just once more flamed up in him anew.

"Why not?" he told himself. "I've got one good race left in me before I'm too old. It'll take two years for this pup to grow big and tough and be trained. I can wait that long. But this'll be my last try at the North American." He said to the pup: "You grow up smart and tough and mean. Not mean like the wolf. Mean like Kävik, the wolverine. He's the meanest in all the North. Grow up like him. Then we'll see what we can do."

The pup growled all through this inspection, and showed his teeth. His big yellow eyes never left the man's face. It was the man who finally looked away. He abruptly dropped the pup. "Go on, get big," he said, and watched the pup struggle away through the long grass.

In the months that followed, Kävik fulfilled all of Charlie One Eye's predictions. He grew big, strong, and smart. Charlie saw to it the wolf side of his nature was not neglected. "A lead dog's gotta be a fighter," he insisted. "Got to lick every dog in the team to keep 'em in line." He showed Kävik no sympathy or mercy. The dog never heard a kind or encouraging word or felt the touch of a gentle hand. Kävik took out his anger at Charlie on the rest of the team. This was as Charlie One Eye wanted.

It was not that Charlie was deliberately cruel. Dogs were machines to do his bidding, and he was training them for the grueling race he knew the North American to be. Properly trained, they could be the answer to a dream he'd had for many years. So he used the whip, and sometimes his feet or a club, unsparingly when they did something wrong. Day after day he ran them until they staggered and were ready to drop. He forced them to pull loads of logs and ice until they could not budge another pound. He made them lean and tough and mean. And Kävik was their leader.

To Kävik all humans were like Charlie One Eye. A truce existed between the man and the dog. Kävik recognized Charlie's authority, but he was not broken or cowed by the man's rough treatment.

At full growth Kävik could travel all day on one small fish. He looked like a big arctic wolf with his grayish-white coat, his black-masked face, and huge head tapering down to powerful jaws and knife-sharp teeth. His legs were long and heavy, his feet broad. His chest was wide, with massive muscles that gave him great pulling strength and amazing stamina. He moved with quick, gliding steps, big head down, yellow eyes slightly narrowed, as if he measured an opponent for a lightning attack. The little trick he had as a pup of looking Charlie straight in the eye he had never lost.

Charlie kept Kävik chained when not working, for to let him free was to invite disaster. Local dogs had challenged him when he ran free, and he killed several with brutal speed.

This was the manner of dog Kävik had become when Charlie One Eye took the team to Fairbanks for his last try to win the North American Sled Dog Derby.

Fairbanks was in the grip of electric excitement. Teams had come from all parts of North America to compete for the richest cash prize ever offered. Charlie had realized all odds were against him and his untried team, and the betting bore that out. But he knew what Kävik could do. He had banked everything on his big, tough leader, and Kävik did not let him down.

This was the dog George C. Hunter saw when he stepped out the door of the Hunter Enterprises Office on Fairbanks' main street just in time to witness the finish of the race. He saw the winning team stagger across the finish line, and collapse, the driver folding over the sled, exhausted. Then the hysterically happy, shouting crowd surged around them. Cameras snapped and whirred, horns blew, people shouted and laughed. A half-dozen public-address speakers blared the time and the winner's name into the bedlam.

This scene was not new to Hunter. It was the same every year.

He was about to turn away when the crowd parted and he again saw the team. Every dog but one was flat on the snow. The leader stood, head up, sharp ears pricked forward, utterly oblivious of the noise and the crowd milling about him. He had the dignity of a king, the bearing of a champion. In spite of the murderous miles he had just run, he looked alert and ready to lunge forward again at the command of his master.

For a surprised moment Hunter thought, Why, he's a wolf!

But no wolf could lead a dog team. This dog did have the heavy legs, the lean-muscled body of a wolf.

"What an animal!" Hunter marveled under his breath. He moved into the street for a better look.

People were fussing over the rest of the prostrate team, unhitching them, petting them, and trying to lift them up on wobbly legs. But no one went near the big leader. He stood alone in a small cleared space, his air of aloofness and calmness unchanged.

Hunter came to a stop an arm's length before the wolf-like dog. The dog dropped his head in a typical wolf's gesture and looked back at Hunter with yellow eyes. So steady was the animal's gaze, the man had the odd sensation the dog was measuring him. The feeling annoyed him, and he tried to beat the dog's gaze down with his own sharp black eyes. The absurdity of the situation came to him, and Hunter turned abruptly away. But as he quit the street, he had the uncomfortable feeling those yellow eyes were boring into his shoulder blades.

A thought came to him, and he stopped to let it work its surprising way through his mind. Once it had, he acted upon it immediately. He strode to where his mine manager stood watching the crowd, and asked, "John, was that the owner pushing the winning team?"

"Charlie One Eye, Mr. Hunter? Sure."

"Where can I find him—away from here?"

"He's staying temporarily in a cabin outside town about a mile. It's right on the road. You can't miss it. There'll be a lot of dogs staked out around the place."

"He doesn't live around here?"

"He's from up Kotzebue way. He'll be heading home in a day or two, I imagine."

George Hunter nodded. He turned, eyes searching for the wolflike dog again. He got only a glimpse; then the crowd surged in front of him. But the dog was standing as calm and impassive as ever.

Charlie One Eye was out in the yard checking over his staked dogs the next morning when George Hunter arrived in an old beat-up taxi. Hunter wasted no time.

"Saw you win the race yesterday. It was quite a show." His voice was sharp and businesslike. He pointed at Kävik staked to a chain some distance from the other dogs, watching him with that level yellow gaze. "I want him."

"You wanta look at 'im? There he is."

"I want to buy him."

"Buy him! That dog?" Charlie's one good eye opened wider.

"That's right."

"You gonna sponsor a team, Mr. Hunter?"

Hunter shook his head. "Got no taste for it; stupid sort of sport. I'll have him sent Outside to my home."

Charlie One Eye rubbed his long jaw while he absorbed

this surprising information. "I really hadn't figured to sell Kävik," he said finally. "He's my lead dog."

"Start figuring now."

The thought of selling a dog to George C. Hunter pleased Charlie tremendously. It would be a real feather in his cap, almost as great as winning the North American. But he knew Hunter's reputation, and became wary. Beneath that small, dapper exterior lurked a very tough man. He'd heard how those black eyes could become glacier cold and his voice icy. By sheer drive, toughness, and shrewdness Hunter had become one of the North's wealthiest men. His mining, fishing, and lumbering interests were extensive. If he sold Hunter a dog he didn't like, the little man would make him no end of trouble. He said, "Kävik's no house dog, no pet, Mr. Hunter."

"That's obvious. What's his bloodlines?"

"Part malamute, part wolf."

"Part wolf?" Hunter seemed pleased. "He looks all wolf."

"He's a quarter, a throwback to a big arctic wolf father. He's got the arctic wolf's eyes, his cunning and strength—his meanness, too."

Hunter kept looking at the dog as if he hadn't heard. "What did you call him?"

"Kävik." Charlie pronounced it Kah-vik. "It's Eskimo for wolverine."

"Odd name for a dog."

"It fits him," Charlie said. "I never tried to make a pet of him. I've been mighty rough on him to make him the kind of lead dog I wanted. You saw it pay off yesterday. I'd rather sell you another dog, Mr. Hunter. I've got some good ones here."

"Can a man handle him? Could I handle him?"

"Sure. He's been trained to handle. But like I said, Kävik's no family pet. He's never been inside a house in his life or had anybody make a fuss over him. He's a sled-dog leader pure and simple. Now, I've got another dog here—"

"I want this one."

Charlie One Eye thought fast. Why did Hunter want Kävik? Then he thought he knew. Hunter collected objects of interest in the North and sent them home. Hunter wanted the animal to show off. Kävik was a dog bred of the wild, part wolf. The very traits he'd been pointing out in Kävik as undesirable were the things the little man wanted. Now that he had made up his mind about this, Charlie decided. The only thing left to do was bargain as shrewdly as possible.

"Give you five hundred," Hunter said sharply.

Charlie shook his head. "His first batch of pups will bring more than that."

"Seven fifty. That's a good price for a dog."

"Not for this dog. He just won the North American. Every racing club from Maine to Mexico will know about Kävik in a week."

"Then name your price."

Charlie One Eye hedged. "Like I said, I hadn't planned to sell him. I'll have to train a new lead dog. That takes time. And every dog won't make a big strong leader like Kävik. Fact is, I don't know where I'd find another like him. Then I'll lose his pups that I could sell. . . ."

"Never mind working up to it," Hunter said impatiently. "Name your price."

"Tell you what, Mr. Hunter. Make it two thousand and you've got a dog."

"That's a lot of money."

"He's a lot of dog. You want one that's part wolf, that looks like a wolf," Charlie said shrewdly. "You'll look a long time before you find another like him, if ever. Two thousand, Mr. Hunter."

George Hunter scowled. He started to argue, then thought better of it. "All right. You've sold him."

"When do you want to take him?"

"Smiley Johnson, the bush pilot, will pick him up this noon. He'll fly him out to my cannery at Copper City, where one of my tenders will take him aboard and deliver him to me in Seattle."

"You'd better make it before noon." Charlie pointed at the leaden sky. "We've got a blizzard comin'."

"Johnson knows. The weather station told him. But he's working on his plane this morning. It's his problem."

"You'll need some kind of strong box to put him in. He can chew right through ordinary wood with those jaws. And he'll try. He's never been cooped up."

"Got an iron cage. Johnson had it built to fly out a young polar bear for the zoo a year ago. It'll hold him."

"You had it all figured out before you came out here this morning," Charlie One Eye accused.

"I always figure things out ahead," Hunter answered.

In such casual manner was the course of Kävik's life changed forever.

# chapter 2

KÄVIK DID NOT UNDERSTAND THE CAGE. Charlie One Eye led him up to the odd-looking thing, opened the door, and shoved him inside, slammed the door and padlocked it. Now he twisted about the small enclosure, growling and snarling. He clamped his big teeth on bar after bar, and bit and wrenched. It was no use. He was firmly imprisoned. Finally he lay down and glared out at Charlie One Eye and the blond young pilot, Smiley Johnson.

"He's pretty smart," Johnson said. "That polar bear fought th' cage all th' way down. It didn't take this fellow long to figure out he couldn't bite through those bars. Sure glad they're not wood. I'd hate to have that character loose in th' plane. Are you sure there's some dog in him?"

"Of course. He wouldn't do anything, if he did get loose."

"Maybe not. But I don't like the way he keeps lookin' at me with those yellow eyes. And I don't like the way he clamps down on those bars."

Charlie shook his head. " Scared of a malamute with a little wolf in him; but not scared to fly this tin box in a storm. If you was smart you'd lay over."

Smiley Johnson laughed. "Trouble with you is, Charlie, you're still traveling by dog team. Why, I'll be eating lunch in Copper City in three hours. Come on, let's load this bundle of dynamite."

It took four men to lift the heavy metal crate with the snarling dog inside, and stow it in the back of the plane.

There in the inner dark Kävik crouched in the cage, yellow eyes shining like burning candles. He was worried and uneasy in these strange surroundings. He heard the roar of the starting motor, and the vibration came up through the bottom of the crate like a thing alive. He felt the plane begin to move and gather speed. The motor roar swelled and swelled until it filled all space. Kävik stood up uncertainly and whined softly. He scratched at the bars and once again tried them with his teeth. He turned around several times in his close confines. Finally he lay down with his big head on his forepaws, resigned to whatever terrible thing was about to happen.

The roaring went on, accompanied by a rushing sound like that of wind high up in the trees. The black compartment where he lay felt insecure, and there was a rolling, tossing motion that never quit and would not let him stand. He crouched on the floor of the cage while these strange sounds and sensations ate away at his courage. He had never been cooped up in the dark, in a cage, with no chance to move about, to fight to defend himself, or to run away. He felt helpless and trapped. Fear, as he had never known it, came to him, and he began to whimper.

In time the swaying motions of the ship became sharper, more violent. They were accompanied by the sickening feeling that he was falling. Then, momentarily they would be gone, only to begin again.

After a particularly violent lurch, Kävik scrambled to his feet and tried to stand. In a frenzy of fear he clawed at the iron bars, then chewed on them, until blood trickled from his straining jaws.

The motor roar quit suddenly on a series of jarring coughs. There was the sound of wind screaming along the sides of the plane, and again that sickening sensation of falling. The motor sputtered briefly to life, and the falling ceased. Then the motor died again. There was the feeling of sliding and never stopping, of spinning and falling, falling without end.

There came a sudden abrupt crash that hurled him against the bars with savage force, a thunderous explosion and a blinding light. The cage went hurtling and spinning through space. Kävik let out one long, unbroken wail of terror that was lost in the tortured rending of metal as the plane struck the frozen earth.

Smiley Johnson, Alaskan bush pilot, had come to the end of his luck.

The storm continued to howl over the mountains and down into the valley where the wreckage of the plane was strewn. It spread a white blanket over the tragic scene, and over an iron cage some feet off in which lay the battered, still form of a wolf-gray animal. The big body was pressed tight against the bars, as though with the last of his failing strength he had fought to get free.

When Kävik opened his eyes the blizzard was still raging, and night had drawn a black swirling mantle over the earth. He lay still, not trying to move. He remembered the dark inside the plane, the musty close smell, and the roaring sound that went on and on. He remembered the sensation of falling and the rolling and tossing that would not let him stand.

He raised his head painfully. The air was fresh and clean and laced with the wild, sweet tang of the out of doors. He heard the strident lashing of the wind in the trees, and felt the snow drive hard and fine against his face. The roaring motor sound and the falling sensations were gone. The solidness beneath him was the earth he knew so well. Through the blinding snow he saw the bulk of trees and brush. Once again the free world was all about him. But he was not free. He was still trapped inside the iron cage.

Kävik tried to stand, but could not. All that marvelous strength that had helped him win the North American was gone. His whole body ached, and every breath was a stabbing pain. He rested for a little, then tried again. On the third attempt he made it, but would have fallen had he not leaned against the bars of the cage. He trembled violently, and his hindquarters refused to hold his weight. He sank back to the floor of the cage.

He coiled into a tight ball, as northern dogs always do during a blizzard, and tucked his nose into the thick fur of his belly. In a little while he drifted off. The storm became a remote sound that grew farther and farther away. The aches and pains of his battered body seemed to follow the sounds of the storm, and finally disappeared as once again he sank into deep shock.

All that night the storm howled over the mountains and down into the valley, piling the snow deep. Normally such a storm would not have bothered Kävik. He had often slept out in forty-below weather when snow drifted completely over him to form a cocoon in which he was comfortably warm. But his many injuries and the terrifying crash had thrown him into shock. His normal body temperature was lowered. Now the cold of the blizzard got through the thick, wolf-gray coat. He shook uncontrollably, and his bruised, battered muscles stiffened.

The long, bitter night passed. Dawn came, gray and thin, and the storm still raged. It continued most of the day. Snow drifted through the bars of the cage and partially covered the dog. But not once did he move. Early in the afternoon the wind slacked off; the swirling curtain of snow began to thin. By the middle of the night the storm had blown itself out. A pale moon sailed into an ink-blue sky, and the stars shone with a frosty brilliance. The earth sank into utter stillness, held in the grip of biting cold.

The blizzard had laid a deep blanket over the wreckage of the plane and piled snow up the sides of the iron crate. To any eye the wreck was now only a mound of uneven snow. The cage was a stump or a rock with snow piled high on its flat top.

Kävik awoke late in the day. He did not try to stand or move about. He knew there was no strength left in his big body. He was ravenously hungry. He'd had nothing to eat the day of the race, and only one small fish and a drink of water afterward. His mouth and throat were on fire. He twisted his head and licked snow until his thirst was somewhat satisfied. He raised his head slightly and looked out at the free world so near.

He saw the snowshoe rabbit bound into the clearing a few feet off, then stop. It sat up and studied the odd object in which Kävik lay. A snowy owl ghosted out of the sky, talons spread. It struck the rabbit in mid-leap like a thunderbolt. There was a single agonized cry; then the owl settled onto the snow and tore open the rabbit. Saliva dripped from Kävik's hungry jaws as he watched the owl gorge himself on the warm flesh. After a little he dropped his head again, exhausted by this small effort. He never knew when the owl left.

The long night came with its intense cold and deathlike hush. Dawn brought a pale sun that slid low across the sky but gave no warmth. All day Kävik lay curled in a tight bundle. A plane came over the mountains and dived low into the valley, trailing its thunderous sound directly over the wreck. Near the end of the day a second plane shot the full length of the valley and disappeared toward the sea.

Dark closed over the earth, and the moon and stars came out. They threw long shadows across the snow. A wolf pack howled far back in the hills as it raced down some unfortunate animal's trail. The sound of their voices rose and fell and rose again, riding the frigid silence. Sometime later a pair of coyotes woke the night with a series of shrill yappings.

This valley was rich in game, and the blizzard had driven every living thing to cover. Now they were all out, hungry and searching for food. Woe to any animal without wings or swift feet or powerful jaws or claws to defend itself. The very cage that held Kävik prisoner now saved him from being eaten.

With the dawn two coyotes came out of the brush and stopped to look at the cage. After a time they moved cautiously forward to investigate. They sniffed carefully about the cage. Kävik represented food, and their keen minds told them he was helpless. But the cage kept them suspicious and nervous. Finally, the boldest stretched a paw through, and clawed at the body. So feeble was the life that flickered in the big dog that this failed to rouse him. The coyote next tried to pull him close so he could reach between the bars with his teeth. But he could not move the heavier dog. In time they trotted away in search of easier game.

A snow-white weasel humped across the clearing within a few feet of the cage without stopping. His mind was on other things. A red fox came to the edge of the brush and hung there like a shadow, sharp ears pricked forward while he studied the odd structure with the still form of an animal inside. After a moment he turned and silently disappeared.

The cold sun was dropping toward the rim of the distant mountains when the lynx came. He was a big fellow, and in his prime. A full-grown lynx will fight a wolf and kill it, for he has not only teeth to fight with but four feet studded with razor-sharp claws with which he can rip an enemy to shreds. The lynx was a stranger here, a long way from his

*He reached a tentative paw through the bars, dug razor-sharp claws into the dog's flank, and yanked.*

natural habitat. He had wandered into the valley some time before. Because he had found that it abounded in snowshoe rabbits, his favorite food, he stayed. Along with the other wildlife, he had been driven to cover by the blizzard, and had not eaten for several days. Since the storm he had caught one rabbit. This was not enough to sate the appetite of a full-grown lynx. He was hungry.

The lynx moved through the valley on big fur-padded feet—seeming almost to drift over the deep snow. His tufted ears were pricked forward, and his round yellow eyes glistened as he slipped silently from thicket to thicket in his search for food. In time he came to the small clearing where the wrecked plane and the iron cage lay. He stopped at the edge of the clearing and studied the cage with interest. He saw where the coyotes had beaten a path around the cage, and he saw the still form of a big animal inside. Finally he moved forward, his stub tail twitching.

The lynx stopped a few feet from the cage, and examined it carefully. Then he walked completely around it several times. At last he sat down close to the bars and looked at the still form inside. He couldn't understand why this big animal didn't wake up and run or turn and fight. He reached a tentative paw through the bars, dug razor-sharp claws into the dog's flank, and yanked. He immediately jerked the paw out again, and waited expectantly.

The searing pain roused Kävik momentarily. His big head came up; his eyes flickered open and his lips lifted briefly in a snarl. Then his head dropped again and he lay still.

The lynx reached between the bars again. He was bolder now. He was about to hook his claws into the yielding body and jerk it against the bars where his teeth could reach it when he heard the sound. For an instant he froze, the paw upheld, claws extended. The sound swelled to a thunderous roar that filled the valley. A great white "bird" burst over the treetops and rushed down upon him. He streaked for the nearby thicket in utter terror.

The "bird" passed overhead and disappeared, trailing the sound after it, even before the cat reached the patch of brush. The lynx dived into cover and crouched trembling beneath a cluster of limbs. The "bird" did not return. Deathly silence settled over the valley again. The lynx lay and waited, in no hurry. Once he was convinced it was safe, he meant to return to the crate and the animal inside.

# chapter 3

ANDY EVANS WAS UP BEFORE DAYLIGHT. HE tiptoed about the kitchen, getting his own breakfast and putting up a lunch. This was Saturday, and he had to run his trapline. He hadn't run it since before the blizzard, and it was going to be a rough all-day job after that storm. He needed an early start. This was his second year running the line. Last year he'd made almost five hundred dollars. He hoped to do as well this season.

Breakfast over, he closed the damper on the stove. He stacked the dishes in the sink, got his bottle of matches and shells from the cupboard, and slipped on his parka. He took his rifle and belt ax from behind the door, and was ready to go. Before he left, Andy tiptoed to the bedroom door, and listened. Normally, his father and mother slept late Saturday and Sunday mornings. His father was watchman at the Hunter's Point Cannery, and in winter there was little to do. This morning he heard his father stirring about. Ever since Smiley Johnson's plane had been lost, his father had been rising early and spending all day at the cannery's shortwave radio, keeping in check with the six bush pilots who were combing the country, searching for the downed plane.

Andy quietly let himself out the kitchen door, took down his packsack, stuffed his lunch inside, and slipped the straps over his shoulders. He stepped into his snowshoes and headed off through the deep snow toward the distant valley and his trapline. Fifty yards from the house he stopped and loaded the rifle.

Andy Evans was fifteen. He was rather thin and bony, with brown hair and a scattering of pale freckles across his face. His heavy-boned frame held the promise of a big man. After he had loaded the rifle, he stood a moment, looking at the night scene spread out below him. The moon was just dropping to its bed in the sea. It and the stars threw a soft light over the earth. Against the whiteness of the snow, the scene lay in black relief.

Their home, furnished by the Hunter Cannery, perched on a rise of ground some hundred yards above the sea. He could see the pale ribbon of trail leading down to the dark bulk of the cannery buildings, the long pattern of the dock, and the outreaching sea. A single boat lay at the dock. It was the cannery tender waiting for the dog Smiley Johnson was flying out. A second trail from the house plunged into a black mass of timber on the right. The trail threaded its way through those trees for a mile, and emerged at the end of the one short street of Copper City.

It wasn't really a city, just a collection of houses and a few stores. A half century ago there'd been a big copper mine here, and the town had held a thousand people. The copper ran out some years ago, and the mine was abandoned. So were most of the homes. A hundred or so people still lived here.

"It should be called Fish Town now," Andy's father said. "Everyone who lives here either works in the cannery or seines during the summer."

Andy's father worked in the cannery.

The moon dropped into the sea, and Andy knew daylight was only an hour or so away. He turned abruptly and slogged off across the tundra.

The valley that held Andy's trapline had been punched into the center of a massive nest of snow-covered peaks. The valley was wide and deep; the floor was sprinkled with brush and timber, ideal for fur-bearing animals. The sides were steep, and rimmed with jagged, bare ridges.

By the time the cold sun broke over the mountains and down into the valley, Andy had taken two muskrats and a weasel. He kept going until the sun told him it was near noon, but he took no more fur. He sat on a stump and ate his sandwiches, then went on again. He guessed he was about halfway over the line. It would be long past dark when he returned home this day.

Sometime later he ran onto the lynx tracks. He kept a sharp lookout. A lynx would bring good money, a lot more than all the muskrat and weasels he could take today. He caught another weasel, and began to feel good. It should be a pretty fair payday. The next two traps had been sprung. He reset them. The next three had not been touched.

The sun was dropping toward the jagged rim of the

valley and the night's cold was beginning to set in when he heard the plane. He stopped and watched it race down the valley and pass over him. It was Swede Ecklund's white job. Swede was one of the bush pilots searching for Smiley Johnson.

Andy went on, keeping a sharp lookout for the lynx. He took another weasel. There were two traps to go. The next was empty. One more, then he could head back for home.

He came to the edge of a small clearing, and there was the lynx moving stealthily into the open from the opposite side. His body was crouched, ready to spring. His eyes were fixed on something straight ahead. Andy raised the rifle, and fired. The cat caught the motion, and whirled. Andy saw his bullet kick up the snow beyond. He'd shot an inch over the cat's head. In two lightning bounds the lynx disappeared into the brush.

Andy stepped into the clearing, disappointed that he'd missed. Then he saw what the odd-shaped mound of snow covered. There was twisted yellow metal under that snow. He saw half a blade of bent propeller, and a broken ski dangled at a grotesque angle. He saw a side of metal and bold black letters, SMI, that ended in a great jagged hole. An odd-looking crate with iron bars lay some distance off.

He had found Smiley Johnson!

For a little he just stood there, shocked by the realization. A single thought kept running through his mind: Smiley almost made it. Two more minutes, and laughing, happy-go-lucky Smiley Johnson would have been safe. Two minutes, less than five miles! Finally he looked all about the clearing. There was no sign of life. No human tracks led away from the wreck. The stillness of death was in the frigid air.

Andy forced himself to go to the plane. There he stepped out of his snowshoes and worked his way through the wreckage until he could look through the door's broken window. Smiley was bent double over the wheel as though asleep. He was still strapped to the seat. Without thinking, Andy said in a small, frightened voice, "Smiley, oh, Smiley!" Then he turned quickly away. He was trembling, and felt half sick.

He saw the crate, the tramped-down snow around it, and moved that way. He dropped on his knees and looked in at the still form of the wolflike dog. At first he thought the dog was dead. His eyes were closed, and there was no movement of breathing along his thin sides. Then Andy noticed the flank where the lynx had torn the skin. Fresh blood was oozing from the wound.

Andy removed his mitten, put his bare hand through the bars, and laid it on the dog's head. He was not sure he felt warmth. He ran his hand down the muzzle to the nose. There was warmth there. The dog was alive. But Andy had seen enough in a year and a half of trapping animals to recognize the gray look of death. He sat back on his heels and studied the dog critically. So this was the lead dog of the team that had won the North American Sled Dog Derby at Fairbanks. He didn't look like much now.

Andy knew he'd have to start back immediately and tell his father what he'd found. But he couldn't leave the dog here like this. Night was coming on. By the time he reached home, and his father could get a party together to come up here, it would be tomorrow morning. The dog would never live that long. He'd die. Or some wild animal like the lynx, or that pack of wolves that was running the ridges every night, would somehow get at him and kill him.

It would be better to put the dog out of his misery before he left.

Andy thought of the dog lying helpless and injured, trapped for three days in the cage. At least he should die outside, free once more.

Andy smashed the padlock with his belt ax and opened the cage door. He reached inside, carefully turned the dog, and slid him out head first. Then he lifted the rifle, placed the muzzle against the dog's forehead, and drew back the bolt. He was about to pull the trigger when the dog's eyes opened and he looked at the boy. The blue eyes of the boy and the yellow ones of the dog studied each other. His eyes held the boy's with as direct a gaze as Andy had ever known. Scarcely realizing what he was doing, Andy tilted the rifle muzzle away and eased back the bolt. As though that was what he had waited for, the dog's eyes closed. Andy watched for them to open again. Then he realized they weren't going to.

He knelt there, trying to decide what to do. Until a moment ago the solution had been simple. Then he had looked into those yellow eyes and was no longer sure. Maybe the dog had a chance to live. If he did, he deserved it after all he'd been through. Andy decided he'd have to take the dog home with him. That would be a real job with some five miles of deep, soft snow to plow through. He'd need some sort of sled to put the dog on. Andy studied the cold sky, gauging the daylight he had left: about another hour. It would be very late when he got home. He'd better face the prospect that he might become too tired and have to spend the night out. In subzero weather that was a thing no one deliberately did. He'd never done it, but he was sure he could. He had plenty of matches and his rifle.

Maybe the dog will die on the way home anyway, he thought. If he does, I'll just leave him.

His mind made up, Andy's thoughts turned to something he could haul the dog on. He didn't want to, but he returned to the plane and began searching through the wreckage. He found a four-foot wing tip that had been torn away. It was light, and would make a good sled. Now he needed straps or rope to make a harness for himself and to tie the dog on. There might be some inside the plane. Andy wrenched the door open and crawled inside. He made his way to the back carefully, keeping his eyes from the still figure in the seat. There he found a coil of rope.

Andy cut holes through the thin aluminum wing and threaded the rope through. He made a loop big enough to slip over his shoulders and across his chest. He pulled this makeshift sled to the iron cage.

The dog opened his eyes briefly as Andy carefully worked the animal's body onto the sled and tied it with ropes across the shoulders and hips.

With the dog secured, Andy took up his rifle. He worked the rope across his shoulders and chest, leaned into the loop, and began the long slow miles home.

At the end of the first quarter mile, Andy knew he had tackled a bigger job than he'd thought. The snow was deep, and though the wing section slid easily enough, the dog was heavy.

The pale sun fell behind the ridges, and night spread swiftly across the land. The moon came up and the stars were bright, casting an eerie, soft light over the snow in which the boy could see a surprising distance.

Andy continued his slow pace back down the valley, stopping to rest only when he could go no farther. At each stop he went back, knelt beside the dog, and stroked his head and spoke to him. Several times the dog opened his yellow eyes briefly.

Andy's stops became longer and oftener. After several hours, he realized he hadn't the strength to get home. He'd better look for a place to spend the night before he was too tired to get a fire going and drag up enough wood for the long hours ahead.

He found a spot some minutes later against a down tree. At the big end of the tree he kicked the snow away to make a hollow to start a fire. He gathered dead limbs in the nearby brush and dragged them up. With his belt ax he chopped an armload of sliver from the side of the tree. Luckily, he had cut into a pocket of pitch.

The pitch flamed up with the first match, and he carefully added chips. He broke up the limbs and fed them into the flames until the fire was big and roaring. Then he pulled the broken wing with the dog close to the log. The heat hit the log and bounced back. It made a small pocket of warmth in the freezing cold of the night.

Andy loosed the ropes and felt the dog's nose. It was hot and dry. He guessed that the dog had a fever, and hadn't had a drink for several days.

Andy packed his handkerchief with snow and held it close to the heat and let the melting snow soak the handkerchief. He lifted the dog's head, pried his jaws apart, and squeezed the precious drops into his mouth. The dog could not swallow, and Andy stroked his throat. At last he felt the muscles work once, convulsively. He repeated the procedure several times, and each time he had to stroke the animal's throat.

Andy gathered more wood, and built the fire high. He sat

with his back against the down tree and let the heat soak in. He watched the dog closely, hoping the heat would rouse him. But there was no change. Andy wondered if his folks were worrying, and guessed they were. He wasn't too worried or disturbed. He had his rifle; the fire was big and warm; and there was plenty of wood. The presence of the dog, even in his present condition, wiped out all feeling of loneliness.

Sometime later he heard the wolf pack running the barren ridges high above. Their voices came down into the valley in a series of high, savage notes that echoed and reechoed up and down the valley.

Their sound seemed to get to the dog, or Andy imagined that he moved slightly. The boy tossed more wood on the fire, and the flames leaped up, spreading their light across the snow. He laid the rifle across his knees and leaned over to stroke the dog's head. He said gently, "It's all right. It's all right." But he couldn't tell if the dog heard him or not.

# chapter 4

ANDY WAKENED WITH HIS FATHER'S BIG hand shaking him, his voice saying gently, "Andy. Wake up, Andy. Wake up."

Andy started up, clutching the rifle. The fire had sunk to a bed of glowing coals; the dog lay on the broken wing tip as he had been, motionless. Andy rubbed his eyes. In spite of the freezing cold and the wolves running the ridgetops, he had slept several hours.

His father was saying: "When it was way after dark and you still didn't come home, we got worried. It's awfully easy to fall and break a leg or something."

"I'm glad you came," Andy said. "I was played out. I had to stop."

His father looked down at the still form of the dog, and asked, "Where did you find Smiley Johnson?"

"About two miles back. He came down in a little clearing on the valley floor. He—He's still in the plane. He didn't even have a chance to get out of the seat. I found the dog in an iron crate about fifty feet away. It had been thrown right through the side of the plane."

Kurt Evans shook his head, "Too bad. Too bad. Smiley was a good flier. Too good. He got careless and cocksure. He was long overdue for trouble."

He knelt and looked at the motionless dog. "So this is Kävik, the wild dog that won the North American." He ran a big hand lightly down the dog's body and over the wolflike head. "I'd like to have seen him before this happened. Too bad you dragged him this far. He's almost dead. You should have put him out of his misery."

"I tried to. But at the last minute he opened his eyes and looked at me." Andy searched for words to explain what that look had done to him, but could find none. "If he'd been running or had jumped me, or if he just hadn't looked at me, I could have done it."

"Maybe it's just as well," his father said. "We'll take him in—if he lives to make it that far. Then Mr. Hunter will know we made every effort to save his dog. Well, let's tie him on the sled and get moving."

It took but a minute to fasten Kävik; then his father slipped the rope over his shoulders, leaned his big chest into the loop, and moved off effortlessly. Andy followed, carrying his rifle and packsack. They made the full distance home without a stop.

At home, Andy and his father carried Kävik, still on the wing tip, into the kitchen. They laid him carefully on the floor. Andy's mother said, "What on earth! Where did you get a dog?" She kissed Andy. "You had me worried, staying out this way. Now, get out of that parka. I've kept your supper hot." Her eyes went to Kävik again, then up at Andy's father. She caught her breath and stood perfectly still, her gray eyes wide with shock, as Kurt told her what had happened.

At the end she murmured: "Poor Smiley. He never would believe he couldn't fly through any storm. 'Put wings on the coffeepot,' he used to say, 'and I'll fly it.'" She looked at the dog again. "What are you going to do with him?"

"I'll have to leave him here for a while," Kurt explained. "I've got to go to the airport and tell Swede Ecklund to call off the search, and arrange for a party to go out and bring Smiley in. And I'd better call Mr. Hunter long distance and ask him what he wants to do about his dog."

"Dad," Andy asked anxiously, "what will you tell him?"

Kurt Evans dug big fingers through his short brown hair, and studied Kävik. "I'll have to tell him how he seems to me," he said finally.

"How's that, Dad?"

"Almost dead."

After his father had left, Andy knelt beside Kävik, loosed the ropes about him, stroked his head, and looked anxiously for some change for the better. There was none.

Laura stole glances at her son as she bustled about, getting his dinner on the table. She sat across from him and watched him pick absently at his food, frowning and silent. Finally she asked, "Andy, when did you find Kävik?"

"About three o'clock," he said, not looking up.

"And you're wrapped up in him already."

"I guess so." Andy looked up, his eyes very blue. "I never felt this way about a dog or anything else before." He shook his head, at a loss to explain the sick shock that had rushed over him at the sight of the wreck with Smiley sitting dead in the plane, and Kävik lying in the cage, trapped and helpless. The heavy feeling of death hung over the little clearing. He'd visualized the dog lying there through the blizzard, and the following two days of bitter cold, with no one to care for him and nothing to eat and drink. Wild animals had tried to get at him and rip him to pieces. A great sympathy had welled up in Andy. He ran fingers through his hair with the same gesture his father used. "Maybe I should have put him out of his misery," he said. "But after all he'd been through, I couldn't do it. He was trying so hard to live. He needed all the help he could get."

"Of course." Laura smiled. "I'm glad you brought him home."

Andy finished his dinner, helped his mother with the dishes, and was bending over Kävik again when his father returned.

"What did Mr. Hunter say?" Andy asked immediately.

Kurt Evans looked at his son soberly. "He said, 'Take the dog out and shoot him.' "

"But he's not dead."

"He's practically dead. You were going to shoot him."

"But I didn't. Dad, what did you tell Mr. Hunter?"

"I told him how the dog seemed to me. That he's got broken bones and probably internal injuries. That he's unconscious most of the time. I told him that there's not a veterinary within two hundred miles and that I didn't think the dog would live to be taken that far, if I could find one."

"Did you have to make it sound so bad?"

"I learned long ago that Mr. Hunter wants all the facts, not hopeful guesses and surmises. I gave him the facts as I see them. I'm not exactly an amateur with dogs, you know."

"But Kävik might live," Andy argued. "I didn't think he'd live till we got him home. But he has. And he doesn't look any worse now than when I found him."

"He couldn't, and still breathe!" Kurt said flatly. "It's no use, Andy. Mr. Hunter said what to do, and he expects me to do it. I think he's right." He reached for Andy's rifle behind the door. "I wish I could have given him a promising report. But I honestly couldn't."

Andy knew his father for a gentle, compassionate man who thought things out carefully and slowly. There seemed to be no argument.

Then he thought of one last thing.

"Why can't we have Dr. Walker look at him first?"

"Vic Walker's a medical doctor, not a vet."

"He *is* a doctor," Andy argued. "He can tell us things."

Kurt shook his big head. "Why can't you give up, Andy?"

Laura had sat, slim hands folded on the table, watching her two men argue. Now she said quietly, "Why should he give up, Kurt?"

"Common sense ought to tell him it's no use—and you, too."

"Having Vic Walker look at the dog makes a lot of sense to me. He could make a diagnosis."

"On a dog?"

"He *is* a doctor."

"That's right! A doctor—not a vet," Kurt said half angrily. "He won't come out here to look at a dog. I know Vic Walker."

"I know him too. I think he might come."

Andy, seeing he was getting help, said quickly, "I'll ask him, Dad. And I'll pay it out of my trapping money."

Kurt turned on his son. "Why do you care what happens to this dog? He's not yours."

"I'm sorry for him. If you could have seen him trapped in that cage . . ."

"I feel sorry for him, too—"

"Then why kill him?" Laura cut in.

"Don't start twisting things around," Kurt warned. "What's got into you, Laura? Where's your good sense?"

"Kurt," Laura said gently, "don't you think it's amazing Kävik's lived at all the past three days?"

"Of course. It's the wolf in him that's living."

"Doesn't he deserve the benefit of every doubt, after putting up such a gallant fight?"

Kurt scowled, and shifted the rifle uncomfortably to his other hand. "Vic Walker wouldn't come out here to look at a dog," he repeated.

"It can't do any harm to ask him." Then Laura added her shrewdest clincher: "It would be the final proof to Mr. Hunter that you'd done everything humanly possible."

"Vic'll be in bed," Kurt argued. "It's eleven o'clock."

"No, he won't," Andy was beginning to see a ray of hope. "He usually stays up late reading. He says it's the only time he gets to read any more."

"Well," Kurt rubbed his face uncertainly. "Oh, all right. But don't you give Walker a bad time. Don't make a nuisance of yourself. If he says 'no,' that's it. You come right back home. Understand?"

"I will," Andy promised. He was getting into his parka as he ran for the door.

Dr. Walker was a bachelor. He lived in a neat white house at the end of Copper City's one street. The front part of the house was his office. He lived in the rear.

There was light in his living quarters when Andy pounded on the door.

Dr. Walker, wearing carpet slippers and an old robe, answered the door. He was tall and lean, about Andy's father's age. He had snapping eyes and straight black hair beginning to thin on top.

"Andy! What brings you out this time of night?" His voice sounded grumpy and annoyed.

"Can you come to the house right away?" Andy asked.

Dr. Walker looked at him, then grunted and began slipping out of the robe. "Accident?" he asked.

"Sort of. Can you hurry?" Andy mumbled.

"Happens every time," Walker grumbled to himself. "Can't get sick or hurt in the daytime so they can come to the office. Got to wait till the middle of the night. What's wrong?" he asked, buckling his overshoes. "Your dad hurt?"

"Dad's all right. He—He's with Mother."

"Your mother, eh? What's wrong with Laura?"

Andy just stood there. All his fine courage had leaked away in the face of Dr. Walker's forbidding manner. He feared if he told the doctor that he was taking him out to see a dog, he'd never go.

Dr. Walker didn't seem to notice Andy's hesitation. "Laura's always been pretty healthy." He took up his bag. "Let's go."

Outside, there was no chance to talk, and Andy was glad. He was hard put to match the doctor's long swinging legs.

They passed through the dense woods to the house in a matter of minutes. Andy held his breath as they entered the kitchen. Dr. Walker growled at his father, "Kurt, fine time to get a man out. What's wrong, Laura?" He saw Kävik, and turned to Andy, eyes snapping. "You brought me out here to treat a dog?"

"Didn't he tell you?" Kurt Evans asked.

Walker's eyes dug into Andy accusingly, "He let me believe Laura was sick."

Andy looked at his father, "I just said you were with Mother."

"You let me jump to a conclusion," Walker said angrily.

"I didn't know what to say. I was afraid he wouldn't come if I told him it was for Kävik."

"You bet I wouldn't! I've had a long day. I manage to steal a few minutes to read, and what happens? I'm dragged out in the middle of a winter night to look at a dog. A dog!"

Laura said: "Andy should have told you, Vic. He was supposed to. But you can understand why he wouldn't. Now, as long as you are here, would you mind looking at the dog?"

"Yes, I mind!" Walker said shortly. "I'm a doctor. I don't treat mutts, especially mutts that look like wolves."

"This is no average mutt," Kurt said. "This is the lead dog of the team that just won the North American at Fairbanks."

"Well—bully for him!" Walker said acidly.

"This is the dog Smiley Johnson was flying out when he was lost."

Walker stopped. "Smiley's been found? Good!"

"Andy found him. Smiley's dead."

"That's too bad. But the way he flew, it was bound to happen. Where'd he crash?"

"On Andy's trapline up in the valley."

"Kävik's laid out there ever since the crash, trapped in an iron cage," Laura added.

"Quite an ordeal," Walker observed dryly.

"Vic!" Laura said, "this dog has been through an awful lot and he's still alive. I know it's taking advantage of an old friend. But won't you at least look at him?" Walker hesitated, and she added, "What possible harm can that do?"

"Well," Walker finally agreed, "all right." He knelt beside Kävik, opened his bag, and took out the stethoscope. Andy watched anxiously as Dr. Walker listened to Kävik's heart, took his temperature, looked at his eyes, pried open his mouth and examined his gums. He ran his long hands down the dog's flanks, probing gently. At last he sat back on his heels and looked up.

"Well?" Laura asked.

"He's got broken ribs and a broken leg. He's in shock. He can't swallow. His pelvis may be broken and he may have internal injuries that only X ray would show. And he's running a temperature."

"Isn't there anything good?" Laura asked.

"His pulse isn't bad, considering. About the best I can say is that his heart's beating and he's breathing."

"Could a good vet bring him through?" Andy's father asked.

"It'd be nip and tuck. Where'd you find one?"

"I don't know."

"Even if a vet saved him," Dr. Walker observed, "his chances of full recovery are slim. My advice is to put him to sleep. I'll do that if you like."

"No!" Andy cried instantly. "Can't you doctor him like you do people?"

"A vet doesn't doctor people," Dr. Walker said, "and I don't doctor animals."

"I suppose there is a great difference," Andy's mother observed. "A doctor couldn't possibly treat a dog. He wouldn't know how."

"Oh, he could," Walker admitted grudgingly. "We use dogs for lab experiments."

"But that's not like doctoring them, like—like setting broken bones and giving them medicines."

"A broken bone's a broken bone," Dr. Walker said. "As for medicines, some are interchangeable."

"I didn't realize the treatment of people and dogs is so much alike."

"Most people don't." Dr. Walker replaced the stethoscope in his bag, closed it, and rose.

Laura continued, following her line of reasoning, "But you'd put Kävik to sleep. If Andy were injured in the same way Kävik is, you'd let him die?"

"Don't sound stupid, Laura," Walker said sharply. "There's a lot I could do."

"Then do it for Kävik," Laura said quietly.

Dr. Walker looked at her a long moment, his sharp eyes boring into her calm face. He shook a long finger at her, and growled positively: "You don't trap me like that! There's more to this than just treating a dog. Suppose this town should learn I'd used the same medicines, the same instruments to operate on this dog that I use on their wives and husbands and kids? The fact that everything is sterilized would make no difference. If I used medicines and instruments meant for humans on a dog, pretty soon they'd be asking which certificate I had—one to practice on dogs and cats or one for people. They'd crucify me, run me out of town."

"I hadn't thought about that," Andy's father agreed. "Folks up here wouldn't stand for it."

"Then take care of Kävik here," Laura suggested.

Dr. Walker shook his head. "He needs intravenous feeding, X ray for internal injuries. He should be checked every couple of hours. Somebody'd start asking why I was coming out here so often. Just forget the whole thing, Laura. It won't work."

Andy knew his mother wasn't listening. She was biting a fingernail thoughtfully. "Victor," she mused, "your house sits at the end of the street, almost up against the trees, doesn't it?"

"You know it does."

"That trail we take to town comes out practically at your back door. Kurt and Andy could take Kävik through the woods and into your house without being seen. You could fix up a place for him in the back room and you'd have him there where you could do all the things necessary and look in on him whenever you liked. No one need ever know. When Kävik is well enough, Kurt and Andy can bring him home the same way."

Dr. Walker was shaking his head emphatically all through Laura's plan. The moment she finished, he said, "That's a crazy idea. No!"

"You mean it wouldn't work? Or you can't do anything for Kävik?"

"Oh, it might work."

"Then you can't do as much for Kävik as you could do for Andy. You're not making sense."

Dr. Walker towered over Andy's mother and shook a finger under her nose. He drew an angry breath, then let it out slowly and stood looking at her. "Laura!" he said finally, "I never won an argument with you, even when we were kids. Now I know why. You've got it all plotted out. You know every move. You know the end before you start an argument. You're not honest. I'm glad you married Kurt and not me."

Andy's mother smiled. "Then you'll do it?"

He continued to glare at her. Finally he threw up his hands. "All right! Anything to get you off my back." He turned to Andy's father: "You fellows carry the dog on that wing slab, and don't shake him around or jolt him. And don't let the whole town see you. I'll go home and have the back door open."

Kurt Evans said, "Vic, you said the dog's chances for a full recovery are slim."

"Something less than fifty-fifty."

Kurt turned to Andy, his face grim: "You hear? Mr. Hunter won't have a cripple. If at any time Dr. Walker says he's not going to make a full recovery, we destroy him. No arguments, no nothing. Still want to try to save him?"

Andy looked at Dr. Walker, a grim, still angry man. He swallowed hard, and nodded, "Yes," he said. "Yes."

Dr. Walker turned to leave, then stopped. "If anybody here so much as breathes one word of this," he warned, "I'll haunt the three of you till Judgment Day!"

"Victor," Laura said.

"Now what?"

"Thank you."

Dr. Walker grunted. He gave her his sourest look, jammed on his hat, and went out without a word.

# chapter 5

WHILE COPPER CITY SLEPT, ANDY AND HIS
father carried Kävik through the dark woods and into the
back door of Dr. Walker's house. Dr. Walker had fixed a
pallet with an old blanket in a corner of the room off his
kitchen. They put the dog down carefully and untied the
ropes from about his body.

Andy's father asked, "Do you want us to stay and help?"

"I'll take it from here. I want both of you out of here—
now!"

"Vic, we appreciate this. We really do."

"Sure! Sure! Now get, will you?"

Andy stroked the unconscious Kävik's big head, and
asked Dr. Walker, "Can I see him tomorrow night?"

"Make it late," Dr. Walker said. "The later, the better.

If there's a light in the office, don't come in because I'll have a patient. Wait until the light's in the back here. And for Pete's sake, be careful. If somebody sees you coming and going out my back door every night, they'll start to wonder."

"I'll be very careful," Andy promised.

"Don't expect too much," Walker warned. "I'll do all I can, but I'm only human."

"Yes, sir," Andy said. "I know."

Andy and his father peeked out the kitchen door, saw all was clear, and went hurriedly across the yard into the black protection of the trees.

When Andy slipped through the doctor's back door late the following night, he was sure, for a sick minute, that Kävik was dead. The dog lay as if he had never moved, his eyes closed. There was a cast on one front leg, as well as a white patch on his flank where the lynx had torn him. A bottle was fastened to the back of a chair, with a tube running down to the dog's leg. The liquid in the bottle was half gone. It seemed to Andy's anxious eyes that Kävik looked thinner, weaker than ever.

"He's still alive," Dr. Walker said. "He's got three broken ribs, but luckily none of them punctured a lung. His front leg is broken; his pelvis is broken. There's a hole on his other side as big as a fifty-cent piece where a piece of metal stabbed almost completely through him. He's lost a lot of blood."

"Is he going to live?" Andy asked fearfully.

"I'm not sure yet."

Andy knelt beside Kävik and began stroking his head gently. Dr. Walker picked up a book, sat in an old rocker under the light, and began reading. From time to time he glanced at the boy. Finally he closed the book and said gruffly: "I've done all I can for him. The rest is up to him and nature. But he's got one big thing in his favor."

"What's that?"

"He's part wolf. That gives him a toughness an all-dog doesn't have. Anyway," Dr. Walker grumbled, "he'd have to be tougher than whalebone to live through your horsing him up on that chunk of plane wing and then dragging him through the snow."

"I was very careful," Andy said. "I eased him out of the cage and slid him on the wing. I didn't lift or pull him. I didn't tie him tight on the wing either, just tight enough so he wouldn't slide off. And I didn't jerk when I pulled the wing through the snow. I did give him a drink. Maybe I shouldn't have."

"How'd you do that?"

Andy explained how he'd packed his handkerchief with snow, let it melt, and then dribbled the few drops from the soaked handkerchief into Kävik's mouth.

"Giving him a drink was good. You're sure he swallowed?"

"I stroked his throat, like this. I felt him swallow."

Dr. Walker's dark eyes studied the boy. "Did you have first aid in school?"

"We've never had such a thing."

"Hm-m-m." Walker opened his book and began to read again. After a minute he glanced at Andy, and muttered again, "Hm-m-m."

Several minutes later the bell rang on the office door. Dr. Walker put aside his book with a sigh. "Somebody with a bellyache," he grumbled. "You be quiet in here."

Andy sat stroking Kävik's head and watching the liquid

from the bottle trickle slowly down the tube into his body. A minute later Dr. Walker came into the kitchen. "That crazy Gabby Nelson ran a sliver in his hand this time of night." He shook his head.

"I'd better go." Andy rose. He stood looking down at the wasted figure of the dog. The breath of life barely stirred his sunken flanks, and not once tonight had he looked at Andy. Andy's eyes followed a drop of liquid from the bottle, down the tube where it disappeared into the dog's vein. By so little was his life held. A wave of despair rushed over Andy, and he said in a thick voice: "He's going to die. I know he is." He turned and went quickly out the door.

But Kävik did not die. There was nothing soft or flabby in his makeup. He clung to the slender thread of life with a tenacity only a half-wild creature, raised and toughened to the trail by a man such as Charlie One Eye, could know.

Each night Andy was relieved to find Kävik still alive. He watched as the bottle slowly fed the precious life drops into the dog's bloodstream. But Kävik didn't move or open his eyes. It was on the third night, when Andy knocked softly on Dr. Walker's door and was admitted, that he found Kävik's eyes open and the bottle and tube no longer attached to him.

"He's going to live, isn't he?" Andy asked happily.

Dr. Walker permitted himself a faint smile. "He'll live. But he's not out of the woods yet."

Andy knelt beside Kävik, and reached out to stroke his head. As the dog's eyes watched the hand, he seemed to try to draw away, but was too weak.

"He's not used to being petted or handled," Dr. Walker said. "All he knows about a hand is getting belted by it."

Andy let his fingers touch the sharp pointed ears, stray

down, and scratch gently at their roots. "What do you mean, he's not out of the woods?"

"I don't know if he's going to make a full recovery."

"How can we tell when he has?"

"If he doesn't limp on that front leg, if the pelvis heals properly, and if his back legs get strong again."

Andy continued scratching lightly at the base of Kävik's ears. It seemed to him that the dog relaxed a little. "When will you be sure?"

"How should I know?" Dr. Walker shook his head, annoyed. "You're the darnedest kid for rushing things. I told you, nature would have to do the job. That it'll take time."

"I just want him to be all right."

"Sure. Sure." Dr. Walker went to the cupboard, took out the remains of a roast, cut off a handful of small pieces, and handed them to Andy. "Here, feed him."

"He can eat now?"

"Of course. That's why I quit intravenous feeding."

Andy held a piece of meat toward Kävik, but the dog pulled his head away and watched him warily.

"Put it on the floor," Dr. Walker said. "He's not used to being hand fed."

Andy put the meat within reach on the floor. Kävik moved his head forward and smelled it carefully. Finally he took the meat, and swallowed it. Andy fed him the remainder piece by piece.

The front doorbell rang, and before Dr. Walker could rise to go into the office the kitchen door opened and little Gabby Nelson stood there. His name was really Henry, and everyone said he was not too bright. But to Copper City he was Gabby because he was always repeating everything he knew. He held out his bandaged hand and said, in a high, squeaky voice, "Doc, you said to come back t'night so's you could look at this. Remember?"

Dr. Walker tried to move between Gabby and the open back-room door so he couldn't see Kävik. Andy reached for the door to swing it closed when Gabby looked around the doctor's lean frame and saw them. He moved into the kitchen and looked at Andy and Kävik. "A dog!" he said. "You doctorin' a dog, Doc?"

"This is a very special dog, Gabby," Dr. Walker said easily, and tried to lead Gabby out of the kitchen. "This is the dog that won the North American at Fairbanks a few days ago. He's a champion, Gabby."

Gabby refused to be moved, and kept looking at Kävik. "You ain't a dog doctor. You're a people doctor."

"That's right. But this is a valuable dog. He needed help or he'd have died."

"But dogs, Doc!" Gabby insisted. "You use th' same knives and scissors and things like that on him you use on me? Medicines too, Doc? I don't like him gettin' th' same medicines I do."

Dr. Walker led Gabby into the office and pointed to a small cabinet. "Everything I use is sterilized in there, Gabby. Everything, understand?"

"Sure, Doc, but usin' 'em on a dog an' givin' people's medicine to a dog." Gabby shook his head. "Town sure wouldn't like it, did it know."

"It's not going to know," Dr. Walker said.

"Sure wouldn't like it." Gabby shook his head gravely.

"Nobody knows but you," Dr. Walker said sternly, "so if the town finds out about the dog, they're going to hear what you've been doing up there in the old mine shaft all these years. You know the whole town will stampede up there, and all your work will be stomped out of sight."

"Aw, now, Doc. You wouldn't," Gabby said, suddenly fearful. "Nobody knows but you. I'm right close t' hittin' a big vein. I know I am."

"Then you'd better be sure nobody hears about this dog."

"I wasn't gonna say nothin'. Honest. You can count on me, Doc."

"All right," Dr. Walker agreed. "As long as nobody learns about the dog, your secret's safe. But not one second longer."

"Okay." Gabby thrust out a grimy hand. "You got a deal."

They shook hands gravely; then Dr. Walker said, "Now come over here and let me look at that hand."

Dr. Walker returned to the kitchen a few minutes later, and Andy asked fearfully, "Do you think Gabby will tell?"

"If he does, he knows I'll broadcast about his activities in the mine shaft. He doesn't want that."

"What's he doing up there?" Andy asked. "Dad says that shaft's been abandoned for years."

"Gabby has the crazy idea he's going to uncover a new vein of copper and that he'll become rich and Copper City will boom again."

"Nobody knows but you?"

"That's what he says. He sneaks up there every dusk and works half the night shoring up the old tunnel and digging new tunnels. He's done an amazing amount of work. I learned about it a year ago when a rock fell on his foot. He couldn't pay his doctor bill, so he told me about the mine and promised me a big stake in his new strike." Dr. Walker stood frowning thoughtfully. "Maybe I scared Gabby enough and maybe I didn't. But he could forget and talk. If he does, I know a few busybodies who'd just love to start snooping and spreading tales. If they discovered the dog, I'd be in trouble. But if they didn't, they'd put it down to more of Gabby's blabbing and forget about it. We've got to get Kävik out of here tonight, Andy."

"Is it safe to take him?"

"I've done all I can. He's getting no medicine now, no intravenous feeding. He just needs a lot of rest and all he can eat. He can get that at your place just as well as here. I'd like to have kept him a couple more days. But it's too dangerous. Get that wing section out of the corner."

They eased Kävik onto the wing tip and tied him securely. Then Dr. Walker and Andy carried him back through the dark trees to the Evans home.

Laura brought blankets and made him a bed in a corner of the kitchen. "He's not used to a house and being around people, so this will be good for him," she said. "No male, man or dog, can resist a woman's kitchen."

"You may be right," Dr. Walker agreed. They eased Kävik off the wing tip and onto the blankets. Dr. Walker said: "All he needs is the usual care, water and food. Let him sleep. He should do a lot of sleeping."

"What if he tries to get up?" Laura asked.

"He won't, until he knows he can. He's smarter than some patients I've had. When he does get up, have Andy come for me. I'll take the cast off his leg, and we'll see how he looks. And, Andy, come at night."

"Then you think he'll make a full recovery?" Andy's father asked.

"I don't know. But we'll get a pretty good idea once he starts moving around."

So Kävik was settled in a corner of Laura's warm kitchen. Every night when Andy came in from school his first questions were: "Has Kävik got up yet? Has he walked?"

"Not yet," his mother would answer. "Remember, Dr. Walker said it would take time."

Andy would kneel beside the dog, stroke his fur, scratch at the roots of his sharp ears, and say anxiously: "He's looking better, don't you think, Mother? I'm sure he's gaining a little weight. His ribs don't stick out so much. He ought to get up soon, hadn't he?"

But Kävik didn't get up. He didn't even try. He continued to sleep long hours, and sometimes he dreamed. Through his mind paraded the events of his short, hard life. There were the shouting and cursing of Charlie One Eye, the sting of the lash, the solid smash of his hard hand. He lived again his countless fights with the rest of the team. He felt the biting cold of forty below when he burrowed deep into the snow for protection. Once more he ran through the brutal months of training, digging in with raw, bleeding feet, pulling until he was ready to drop. For this he had been fed one small fish a day. Hunger was an ache that never left. Over and over he ran the grueling miles of the North American.

But there was one particular nightmare through which he suffered again and again—the terrible ride trapped in the iron cage in the dark interior of the plane. He heard the roaring sound again, felt the slipping, the falling. He went through the horror of the explosion, the burst of light. Then he and the cage would go spinning end over end through space. At such times his muscles jerked, and he whimpered in his sleep. This would bring the woman, and her soft voice and gentle hands would wake him.

At first the dreams seemed more real to Kävik than the kitchen. He had lived through the dreams, but the nearest he had come to being inside a house with people had been his short stay in Dr. Walker's back room. He remembered little of that. Now he was living with people. He heard the cold winter wind bite at the corners of the house while he lay warm on his blanket. His delicate black nostrils were filled with the delicious odors of cooking food. And he ate this food every night from a white bowl. Not once did he taste the half-thawed fish that had been his chief diet for the two years of his life.

Kävik was three-quarters dog, but Charlie One Eye had cultivated the wolf in him. The dog part wanted the companionship, the love, and attention of people. Now these dormant emotions came alive in him.

At first he tried to object to the hands stroking and petting him, but he was too weak. Then he became accustomed to their touch, and soon he was waiting expectantly for it. He knew the different hands without opening his yellow eyes. The man's hands were heavy; his strokes and pats were solid, but gentle. The boy's touch was lighter, but it was sure and smooth, and he spent much more time stroking him. The woman's hands were soft and light. Not once did he receive a stinging cuff followed by shouted commands and curses. These hands stroked and petted, and the voices were quiet and friendly.

Kävik was a young dog, and the time he'd spent under the rough treatment of Charlie One Eye had not yet made his nature permanently harsh and unyielding. He responded to these people, but it was to the boy he gave his love. As Andy's mother said: "It's logical. There's not much difference between a boy and a dog. And considering that a dog's years are seven-to-one in ratio to a human, they're about the same age. It's youth answering to youth."

Each day Kävik waited for the boy's return from school. He would lie head up, ears pricked forward. He could catch the quick crunch of the boy's feet in the snow long before human ears could.

Andy always went straight to Kävik, and knelt beside him to stroke his head and scratch at the base of his ears while he searched for improvement. He would say anxiously: "Seems like he ought to walk pretty soon. He ought to try, anyway. He can't get strong just lying here."

And his mother always answered: "Stop trying to rush it. Dr. Walker said Kävik will know when he can get up."

Kävik would lift his head toward the boy, and his black nostrils sucked in the clean, fresh scent of the outdoors that clung to the boy's clothing. The boy would talk to him, his voice low and intimate, while his fingers went on exploring at the roots of his ears or under his chin. Kävik learned to roll his big head so this marvelous sensation was transferred from one side to the other.

Each night Andy would hold forth some tempting morsel of food and coax him to take it. But for a reason that went back to the first time Charlie One Eye had sent the pup sprawling with that stinging slap of his big hand, he could not bring himself to stretch forth his head and take it. Andy always ended by putting the morsel of food in his bowl, whence it was immediately taken.

Kävik enjoyed most the time after dinner. The kitchen was warm, and the faint aroma of cooking still lingered.

61

The three people sat about the table, taking advantage of the overhead light. The boy would be studying, his brown head bent over books. The man read a paper or magazine, and the woman was usually mending some article of clothing or knitting on a sweater she was making for the man. Kävik would stretch full length, close his eyes, and listen to their low voices and bask in the wonderful feeling of belonging.

After a time the boy would put away his books, get out a comb and brush, and sit on the floor beside him. "All right," he'd say, "time to get beautiful." Then for half an hour he'd brush and comb the dog's wolf-gray coat. Finally the boy would put the comb and brush away, set a pan of fresh water before him, smooth the wrinkles from his blanket, give his big head some final pats, and disappear up the stairs. The older people would stay a while longer. Then the man put out the light, and they followed the boy. Kävik would be alone in the kitchen.

There came a night when the family was eating dinner, and Andy's father was talking about the coming canning season. Andy felt a touch at his arm and looked down to find Kävik at his elbow, balancing shakily on three legs.

Andy yelled: "Dad! Mom! Look, look! He's got up. Kävik's got up!" He put his arms around the dog's neck and looked at his father, his eyes shining, "He can walk, Dad. He's going to make it! He's going to be all right, isn't he?"

Kurt leaned across the table and studied the dog. "Looks promising," he agreed. "We'll see what Vic Walker says."

Andy started up. "I'll go get him so he can take the cast off his front leg. He said to come for him when Kävik got up."

"It's too early," his mother said. "Victor told you to come when it was dark. You eat your supper."

Andy sank back in his chair. Kävik kept looking at him, his tail waving.

Andy took a bite of meat and held it under the dog's nose as he'd been doing every night for days. Kävik licked his lips and looked at the meat, then up at Andy. "Come on," Andy coaxed. "I'm going to keep right on until you take it. You might as well start now." The yellow eyes of the dog and the blue ones of the boy looked into each other. Then Kävik rolled back his lips from the big tearing teeth and reached forward cautiously. He lifted the meat from Andy's palm so deftly the boy scarcely felt it. Andy patted his head and crooned, "That's a good boy. That's good!" He proffered another piece. Kävik took it. Andy reached for a third.

"No, you don't," his mother said. "You eat that. Kävik's had his dinner, and he's stuffed."

Kävik stood expectantly at Andy's elbow for another minute, then hobbled back to his blanket and lay down. That had taken all his strength.

Andy was so excited he scarcely touched his food. His father and mother held him back two endless hours before they finally let him go for Dr. Walker.

After Dr. Walker had examined the dog critically, he said: "He's looking surprisingly good. He's put on weight. He's a mighty tough animal."

They gathered around and watched silently as he carefully cut the cast away.

Kävik lay there for several minutes, as if he weren't sure what he should do. Then he scrambled up. He wobbled uncertainly on three legs, then carefully, slowly put the fourth on the floor. The act seemed to give him confidence. His sharp ears shot forward; his back straightened. He seemed to grow taller and to stand with purpose. He dropped his head in a typical wolf gesture and looked obliquely up at them with yellow eyes.

"Good heavens!" Andy's mother said. "He does look like a wolf!"

"A big arctic wolf," Andy's father said. "A throwback sure."

"Lead him around a little," Dr. Walker said to Andy. "Let's see how he walks."

Andy coaxed Kävik through the kitchen, into the dining room, the living room, and back into the kitchen. The moment he began to walk, all that fine confidence deserted him. His head dropped and his ears flattened. He limped terribly, and when he reached the kitchen again, he collapsed panting on his blanket in the corner.

Andy looked at Dr. Walker fearfully, trying to read his long, sober face as he studied Kävik. Andy's father looked at his feet and said nothing. His mother bit her lips.

Andy knelt and stroked Kävik's head, and waited, scarcely daring to breathe. He could hear Kävik's labored panting and feel his whole body tremble with the effort. He wanted Dr. Walker to say Kävik was going to be all right more than he'd ever wanted anything. But he feared the doctor wasn't going to. The wreck, the injuries, and lying out there in that iron cage in the storm had been more than even his wolf-tough constitution could overcome. He was not making a full recovery. Maybe they should have put Kävik to sleep that first night when Dr. Walker wanted to.

"Sure he's weak and he's got a bad limp," Dr. Walker said. "He's been through a mighty tough ordeal. I told you his chances were less than fifty-fifty. When I got him home and began working on him, I realized they were even less. I wouldn't have given a plugged nickel for his chances that first night." He leaned forward and scratched Kävik's ears. "You're about as tough as they come." He looked at Andy then, and said, "I told you that wolf strain was tough, boy."

Andy's heart almost stopped, then began to race madly. "You mean he's going to be all right? He's going to get well. He'll make a—a—"

"A full recovery?" Dr. Walker asked. "I'd bet on it. Naturally, he's stiff and weak. But with exercise he'll grow strong again. That stiffness will limber up and disappear."

Andy put his head down to Kävik, and murmured: "You hear that? You're going to be all right again."

Kävik sniffed at the boy. Then, for the first time in his life, he ran out his pink tongue and licked a human face.

Dr. Walker snapped his bag closed, and rose.

Andy's father asked, "How much do we owe you, Vic?"

"I said I'd pay it, Dad," Andy said quickly.

"Never mind, Andy. . . ."

"It was Andy's idea to get Dr. Walker," Andy's mother said. "He should pay his own bill."

Dr. Walker looked at Andy. "Where you going to get this money?"

"Out of my trapping money."

"I see." Dr. Walker rubbed his long jaw thoughtfully. "Bring me about five dollars sometime."

"Now, Vic . . . !" Kurt began.

"That will hardly pay for the cast," Andy's mother said.

"You said that was Andy's bill. Then let Andy and me

settle it. Of course that five dollars won't pay the whole bill, not by a long shot," he said to Andy. "But if I know your folks, you're going to college. You just might decide to study medicine. If you do, and some kid brings you a sick dog, see that you take care of him. Understand?"

"Yes, sir," Andy said. "And I'll bring the money to your office tomorrow morning."

"Good enough." Dr. Walker picked up his hat.

"You grouchy old bear," Laura said softly, "you're a fraud."

Dr. Walker scowled at her. "Kurt," he said, "how do you manage to live with this woman?" and left.

After Dr. Walker had gone, Andy coaxed Kävik into two more tours of the kitchen, dining and living rooms, and each time he collapsed panting on his blanket. But it seemed to Andy he was a little steadier the last time. He patted Kävik's head, and said, "You did fine. Just fine." Kävik thumped his tail on the floor and lifted his lips in a grin.

Andy's father said: "You're not forgetting that Kävik belongs to Mr. Hunter. You'll have to give him up, you know."

Andy rubbed Kävik's ears, and the dog laid his head on his knee. Andy kept rubbing his ears. He had forgotten. He'd been so full of wanting Kävik to get well there'd been no room for any other thought. Now it suddenly lay on his stomach like a rock. "When will you tell Mr. Hunter about him?" he asked.

"I'll write him tomorrow and explain everything."

"Do you have to write so soon? Kävik's not clear well yet, Dad."

Kurt's thinking always followed a straightforward, simple

line. Right was right, wrong was wrong, and the truth must always be told. "Mr. Hunter thinks his dog is dead. He should know he's alive and that he's going to recover."

Laura sat nibbling at a fingernail, and now she said thoughtfully: "I don't think you should tell him just yet. Mr. Hunter has accepted the fact of Kävik's death. If you tell him he's alive, he'll want him back immediately. If he sees a thin, scraggly, weak dog that limps badly, he'll get rid of him. It's not fair to Mr. Hunter or to Kävik for him to see the dog now. Kävik won't be fit for a couple of months. In that time the cannery will open for the spring run, and Mr. Hunter will be coming north as usual. Let him see Kävik then, when he again looks like the big strong dog that won the North American."

As Andy watched his father's face, he added anxiously, "Kävik doesn't look very good, Dad."

Kurt scowled at the dog while he thought this through carefully. "All right," he agreed finally. "We'll wait. But don't forget, you'll have to give him up."

"I know," Andy said. He sat there a few minutes longer, stroking and petting the dog. Finally he rose and filled Kävik's water bowl and put it beside him. He straightened the blanket a little; then he said "Good night" to his parents, patted Kävik's head again, and climbed the stairs. The dog watched him out of sight.

A little later Laura and Kurt turned out the light, and Kävik was left in the darkness of the kitchen. He lay for some time looking at the stairway up which the boy had disappeared. Finally he rose laboriously, limped to the foot of the stairs, and looked up.

The boy was up there somewhere. He put a paw on the first step, and began to climb. Lifting his weight up each step was much harder than walking. Soon his legs began to tremble; halfway up, he sat down on the steps, and rested. Then he went on. At the top he faced a short hall with two doors. His delicate nose led him unerringly to the boy's door. The door was ajar, and he pushed it open. He walked across to the bed and put his cold nose against the boy's cheek.

Andy sat up with a start. "Kävik! You climbed the stairs. You climbed the stairs!" He put his hands on either side of the big head and pressed his face against the furry forehead. "You're sure getting strong fast. I knew you would. I knew it!" Kävik waved his tail gravely and licked Andy's face.

"So you want to sleep with me," Andy said. "That's dandy!"

Andy pulled a throw rug on the floor to a place at the head of the bed. He patted it and said, "Come on, lie down. Right here."

Kävik curled up on the rug with a tired sigh. He felt the nearness of the boy in the bed beside him, his hand trailing over the side touching him. The smell of the boy filled his nostrils. This was where he wanted to be.

# chapter 6

NOW THAT KÄVIK WAS ABLE TO MOVE ABOUT, he improved rapidly. In the first couple of days he inspected every inch of this strange house where he'd come to live with people. Laura let him out every afternoon, and he remained out until Andy returned home from school.

Once again Kävik enjoyed the crisp winter air and deep snow. It provided just the sort of violent exercise he needed to build back his strength. He spent his time traveling between the cannery and the house at Kurt's heels, or exploring the slopes behind the house almost to the valley where Andy's trapline began. He was never out of sight of the house for long. He would come limping back through the snow to make sure everything was just as he'd left it.

But Kävik never missed meeting Andy when he returned from school through the dark belt of trees. That time sense, which all animals have and which tells them when important things are to happen to them, told him within a minute or two just when Andy was due. He'd stand in the yard waiting, head up, ears pricked forward expectantly, yellow eyes watching the trail where it emerged from the timber.

The moment Andy appeared, Kävik would let out a glad yelp and go struggling through the snow to him.

He still ate in a corner of the kitchen and begged morsels while standing at Andy's elbow each night. After dinner he would curl at Andy's feet, close enough so the boy could reach down and scratch his ears while he did his homework. But he no longer slept on a blanket in a corner of the kitchen. When Andy climbed the stairs to go to bed, Kävik now climbed beside him. He slept on the rug on the floor at the head of Andy's bed.

In this manner was the memory of Charlie One Eye and the two brutal years of his life wiped out of his mind. These three people and the house were his whole life. It was as if he had never had any other.

Kävik's thin flanks filled out; the sheen returned to his thick, wolf-gray coat; and last of all the limp completely disappeared. Once again he looked like the magnificent animal George Hunter had seen win the North American at Fairbanks.

On the third weekend, Andy took Kävik with him when he ran the trapline. It was still dark. The earth was bathed in the soft light of a half-moon when they crept down the stairs, let themselves quietly out of the house, and went up the slope. All morning Kävik tore through the snow, leading the way. He'd make short side excursions to investigate, then rush back to check on the plodding Andy. He was particularly interested in the traps, and stood close at each set to watch as the boy removed the game and reset the trap.

At noon they ate lunch sitting side by side in the snow in the protection of a log. Andy carefully tore each sandwich in two and fed half of it to Kävik. "I'll bet this is the first trapline you've ever run," Andy said. "Like it?"

Kävik waved his tail, and grinned.

"Me too," Andy said, and ruffled the fur between the yellow eyes. "It gets real lonesome running a line alone."

They came in time to the wreck of the plane and the iron cage. Kävik advanced cautiously. He sat down a few feet from the cage, and studied it. He looked back at Andy, as if asking for an explanation.

The boy said, "You sort of remember, is that it?" As if the boy's voice gave him confidence, Kävik got up and moved closer, then sat down again.

"Go ahead," Andy said; "look at it good."

Kävik moved forward again, thrust out his nose, and sniffed the iron bars.

"See," Andy said, "it can't hurt you." Kävik walked all around the cage, then returned to Andy.

Andy bent and put his arms around the dog's neck. Kävik whined softly and licked Andy's face. "Do you remember that cage?" Andy asked. "Do you know that Smiley was killed here? They say dogs sense things like that. Is that what's bothering you?" Kävik continued to whine, and stayed close to Andy until the boy rose and started up the valley again.

"It's lucky for you I came when I did that day," Andy said. "I guess it was lucky for both of us."

After that first time, they passed the broken plane and iron cage many times, but Kävik never went near them again.

The end of the trapping season came, and with its passing Andy knew that spring and the annual salmon run would soon be here. George C. Hunter would return and find Kävik. Again the rock was in Andy's stomach, and each new indication of spring made it heavier. The daylight hours grew swiftly longer. The first warm breath blew softly across the land, shaking the snow burden from the trees.

The snow began its annual retreat from the beach, back up the hill, past the house, and into the valley. It crept up the valley slopes, then stopped to form a white backbone that stretched along the tops of the high ridges. It would remain there all summer. The green and yellow tundra came into view.

The first ducks and geese arrived while the ponds and streams were still frozen over. Andy and Kävik watched the first big V of geese sail high over the ridgetops, bank, and dip into the valley. They had their look, then tilted upward again and flew on, heading for the nesting grounds farther north. A flight of mallards dived into the valley, heading for a nearby pond. They set their wings and glided in, mistaking the clear ice for water. The whole flight went tobogganing wildly across the ice with startled squawks and flapping wings, and piled up against the far bank. Andy laughed, and Kävik let go a stream of excited barks. The shocked ducks righted themselves, sprang into the air, and fled down the valley in panic.

Overnight the tundra burst into color as tiny flowers pushed through the carpet of moss. Willow and poplar buds opened. The alder thickets, which had looked like huge tangles of dead bare limbs, became a mass of green.

A dozen men flew in from Seattle to overhaul the cannery's machinery and make ready for the season. A pair of early seine boats came in from the south and tied to the dock to await the coming salmon run. The first salmon stragglers fought their way up the tiny stream. The rock in Andy's stomach grew heavier and heavier.

School let out for the summer. The next day Andy went to town to look for a job. During fishing season every man in town, who could get away, went seining. This left vacancies in the local stores. Andy figured that this year he was old enough and big enough to fill one of these temporary openings.

For the first time he took Kävik with him. They walked the full length of the town's one street to Tom Murphy's hardware store. This would be a good place to start. Murphy's son, Bob, who worked in the store with his father, had gone seining last summer.

Mr. Murphy scratched his head, and said: "Bob's out right now, trying to contact the skipper of the *Lady Claire*. That's the boat he was on last year. If he gets it, he'll go. Come see me again tomorrow, Andy." He leaned over the counter, adjusted his glasses, and looked down at Kävik. "That's quite a dog you've got there. Or is he a dog?"

"He's part wolf," Andy said proudly. "His name's Kävik. It means wolverine."

"Hm-m-m," Mr. Murphy said. "Seems like I heard that name somewhere."

"He won the North American at Fairbanks," Andy said. "He—He's Mr. Hunter's dog."

"Sure. I remember. Well, you come see me tomorrow, Andy."

On the street again, they were passing the Alaska Bar when Pinky Davis, the bartender, hailed Andy. Andy had always liked Pinky. He was short and fat and jolly. Now he stood in the Alaska's doorway with several seiners, and called, "Hey, Andy, where'd you get the wolf?"

Andy stopped in the middle of the dirt street and said: "He's only part wolf. He's the lead dog that won the North American."

"That's the dog Smiley Johnson was flyin' out for Hunter?"

"Yes," Andy said. "His name's Kävik. It means wolverine."

"That so," Pinky said, and he and the seiners looked on Kävik with approval.

A half-dozen dogs swung into the far end of the street and trotted forward in a tight pack. They were all local mongrels that seemed to belong to no one, and they scrounged their living where they could. As a pack they terrorized every cat and every other dog in town. They were led by a big, ungainly houndlike mongrel name Blackie.

Blackie spotted Kävik, and stopped. Here was an outsider, a stranger, and to add incentive, an animal that looked like a wolf. Blackie plunged forward, bawling at the top of his voice. The whole scrubby pack howled at his heels.

Kävik waited until they were almost upon him; then he

74

whirled suddenly, and, tail between his legs, dashed into the opening between the Alaska Bar and Murphy's Hardware. The pack charged into the opening after him. They cornered him against a high fence, and Blackie rushed in, struck the cringing Kävik, and bowled him over. He leaped upon Kävik, big jaws sprung wide. Kävik dodged Blackie, charged through the rest of the milling pack and out into the street again. A small long-haired dog, too slow to keep up with the pack, was just arriving to join in the fight. He charged into Kävik on short legs, got hold of a flying hind leg, and bit down. Kävik shook the small dog off with a frightened yelp of pain, raced the full length of the street with the pack in howling pursuit, and vanished among the trees, heading for home.

"Well, holy mackerel!" Pinky Davis looked at the men around him. "Did you see that? Why, the little old Rags even took a bite outa him and he wouldn't fight back." He looked at Andy. "What'd you say his name meant? Wolverine? You sure it ain't rabbit, Andy?"

"Couldn't be a rabbit," one of the seiners said seriously; "a good healthy rabbit'ud kill 'im."

Andy turned without a word and went blindly up the street, the laughter following him. He felt sick and bewildered and fighting mad. He'd like to take a club to that fat little Pinky Davis and his friends, and to that whole pack of dogs—especially Blackie. Oh, especially Blackie!

Andy found Kävik crouched far back under the front porch in the dark. He coaxed him out and patted his head and scratched at the roots of his ears. "What's wrong with you?" he asked gently. "You could have licked that big Blackie easy. Then the rest would have left you alone. And that little mutt of a Rags. You could eat him in one bite.

Why'd you run away like you were scared to death? You did act like a rabbit. Why? Why?" Kävik's ears were laid flat to his big head, and he whined pleadingly while his tail thumped the ground hopefully. "I don't understand," Andy said miserably. "I just don't understand."

He took Kävik into the house with him. The dog went to his corner of the kitchen and lay down and looked disgraced. The dishes and food were on the table. Andy's father had just finished his lunch and was slipping on his coat in preparation to go back to the cannery. He looked down at Kävik, and asked, "What's wrong with him?"

"That bunch of dogs in town," Andy said angrily. "That Blackie . . ." He told them what had happened. His father just stood there looking down at Kävik. "So he didn't make a complete recovery after all," Kurt Evans said.

"But he's well and strong," Andy insisted. "You said yourself he couldn't look better."

"Physically he made a fine recovery," his father agreed. "But here"—he tapped his chest—"he didn't make it. He's lost his confidence and courage."

"How, Dad?"

"Probably the plane wreck. He sustained injuries that would have killed any other dog. Then he lay out there in the storm all that time, more dead than alive. It knocked all the fight out of him."

"You said, if he didn't make a complete recovery . . ." Andy began fearfully.

"I was thinking physically. He's made it physically."

"Will Mr. Hunter want him like this?" Andy asked.

*They cornered him against a high fence . . .*

"No," Andy's mother said positively.

"Then maybe Mr. Hunter will sell him to me," Andy said hopefully.

"You wouldn't mind that every dog in town can run him ragged?"

"I'd mind. I just won't take him to town. Do you think he might sell Kävik to us, Dad?"

"He might. A coward would be as distasteful to Mr. Hunter as a physical cripple. And no one else up here will want him. Selling him to you for anything he can get would be a way to recoup a little of his loss."

Laura nodded. "That's how he'll look at it." She smiled at Andy. "I think you're going to have a dog."

"It all depends on Mr. Hunter," Kurt said.

"When he comes, you'll tell him how Kävik is?"

"I'll tell him," his father said grimly. "Mr. Hunter wouldn't take kindly to learning the sort of dog he's become after he'd taken him home."

Andy looked at Kävik, and said with helpless anger: "He even ran away from that little old Rags. It doesn't make sense."

"It makes sense."

"When he's five times bigger, a part-wolf lead dog?" Andy pointed out. "What's he got to fear from that little mutt?"

"It's not really fear. It goes much deeper."

"All I know is, he ran away like he was scared to death," Andy said.

His father studied him a long moment; then he said quietly, "Sit down, Andy. I'll try to explain."

Andy slipped into a chair. His father sat across from him and said: "Andy, I've wanted to tell you something for

78

some time, but I didn't know how to make it clear to you. Now maybe I can."

"What's that, Dad?"

His father looked at his clenched hands, and said, "Haven't you wondered why I'm working as a handyman around the cannery and as watchman in winter, when I was once one of the top seiners in the North?"

Laura said in a sharp voice, "Kurt!"

"It's time he understood," Evans said deliberately. "If he hasn't asked himself already, he soon will. And now that he's older, he'll be getting around these fishermen more. He'll hear talk, and he should have it straight. Andy's not a child anymore."

Andy's mother looked from one to the other of them, biting her lips. Then she turned abruptly and left the room.

Kurt Evans looked at Andy, and Andy said, "Boats cost a lot of money."

His father shook his head. "That's only part of the reason. Several people have offered to finance me. Mr. Hunter tried to get me to take the *Hustler*, that big seiner he has lying at the dock. I've said no every time." His father rubbed his hands together with a faint nervousness. "That's where Kävik and I are so much alike."

"How do you mean, Dad?"

"Remember when we lost our own boat, the *Freedom*, five years ago?"

"I remember," Andy said.

She had struck a rock in the fog, and sunk. Two crewmen and his father's brother, his Uncle Eddie, had been lost. Before it was over, their home and all his father's and mother's savings were gone.

"That night," his father said quietly, "I lost my confidence. I'm not physically afraid. But a man can take such a beating he loses the desire to try again. The heart is knocked out of you. You're empty. That something you should have—that makes you want to fight—is gone."

Andy felt sick and shocked at hearing his father talk so. He suddenly wanted to protect him, to make excuses. He said, "But, Dad, it likely wouldn't happen again."

His father nodded. "I know that. But there is always the possibility. It's one of the hazards of seining, especially in these waters. In the past five years your mother and I have managed to save a little. We want our own home. You've got college ahead of you. It would all be wiped out if it happened to me a second time. I tell myself I can't take that chance. But there's more to it than that. I simply don't have the desire to make a fight of it."

"And it's something like that with Kävik?" Andy asked. "The plane crash, almost being killed, then lying in the cage for days knocked all the fight out of him?"

"That's about it. He finds it easier to run away than to put up a rousing fight. Nothing is driving him to make the effort. It's easier for me to go along as I am, saving a little, getting our home, putting you through school, being secure —than to take any chance, however slim it might be."

"I see," Andy said. And he really did.

"But you still want Kävik, if Mr. Hunter will sell him?"

"Yes."

"All right. I'll see what I can do." His father rose.

"Dad," Andy asked, "will it always be this way with Kävik and . . ." He bogged down, embarrassed.

"With Kävik and me?" his father finished. "With Kävik I'd say Yes. For myself . . . I don't know. I just don't know." Then he went out and down the trail to the cannery.

Andy got the job at Murphy's Hardware. Every morning when he went to work Kävik accompanied him through the trees to the edge of town, and there he stopped. Never again did he venture into the street. He stopped well back in the trees where he could not be seen. Andy would pat his head and scratch his sharp ears and say: "I've got to go to work now. You'd better go back home." Kävik would watch him enter the street, then turn and trot back down the trail.

Pinky Davis didn't let Andy forget Kävik's experience with Blackie and the town dogs. Whenever Pinky saw Andy he'd sing out, "Andy, how's the rabbit?" or, "When you gonna bring th' rabbit to town again? We ain't had a good race down Main Street in some time. Maybe next time we can sell tickets or take bets, huh?"

Andy never answered Pinky Davis. He looked straight ahead and marched past the Alaska Bar, his jaw set and his lips pressed tightly together. But he vowed that someday, somehow, he'd get even with Pinky.

At night Kävik always waited in the fringe of trees for him. The dog's time sense was amazingly accurate. He never missed. He'd be standing in the middle of the trail, his bushy tail waving as he did a little dance step with his front feet to show how happy he was to see Andy.

Andy would kneel in front of him so Kävik could put his big head against the boy's chest while Andy scratched his ears and talked to him. "Did you have a good day?" he'd ask. "Did you go to the cannery with Dad?" Then he'd tell

Kävik about his day. "I didn't do much. I don't know why Mr. Murphy keeps me around. Everybody's out fishing." Or ,"That Pinky Davis! Someday! Someday!" Then he and Kävik would race home through the trees together.

Andy had never had a pet to love before, and Kävik had never been loved or given his love. Now each was discovering how wonderful their companionship could be. Andy had stopped worrying about Mr. Hunter's eventual arrival. He was convinced that Mr. Hunter would never want Kävik once he knew what a coward he was. And to ease his mind further his father and mother were equally convinced. His one remaining problem was, How much would he have to pay for Kävik? And again his reasoning, and that of his father, told him, not much. "Who else would want him?" his father asked. "A dog that's a coward is no good up here."

The short seining season was half over when Andy, heading home one night, found no Kävik waiting for him in the fringe of trees. He looked about for several minutes, whistling and calling. Blackie and his pack heard the whistling, and padded down the street to investigate. Andy picked up a club and hurled it at them. Blackie stopped, and the pack stopped behind him. Andy picked up another club and started forward. "You want a fight," he said to the big black dog, "I'll give you one." Blackie swung about with a disdainful toss of his head and started down the street. The pack fell in at his heels. Rags, the little feist, trotted in the rear, his short legs pumping to keep up.

Andy dropped the club and turned toward home. Maybe Kävik had gone to the cannery with his father and had forgotten the time. But he never had before. Or maybe Blackie and his pack had discovered him waiting here in the trees and had chased him home. He bet that was it. One of these days he'd get even with that Blackie. He'd get him good!

Dinner was on the table when he walked in, and his father and mother were waiting for him. Kävik was not lying in his corner in the kitchen. "Where's Kävik?" he asked. "He wasn't waiting for me."

Andy's father looked at him and said nothing.

"Mr. Hunter was here right after lunch," his mother said gently.

"Oh." Andy looked at his father. "You talked to him about Kävik? You told him how he was? How much does he want for him?"

Andy's father shook his head. "He took him, Andy."

"Took him! You mean Kävik's gone?" Andy's voice was high and a little sharp. "You said he wouldn't want him. You said we could buy him."

"I said I didn't think he'd want him," his father said patiently. "Well, I was wrong."

"Did you tell him how he was? That he won't go to town because he's afraid of the other dogs? That even that little feist, Rags, can chase him? Did you tell him, Dad?"

"I told him, Andy. I even offered to take him downtown with Kävik and let the dogs chase him to prove it. He just stood there and smiled and didn't believe me. He thought I was just making up a story so he wouldn't want his dog and we could keep him. I can't blame him for thinking that. Kävik looks wonderful, as you know. Big, healthy, and strong. He looks like the Kävik Mr. Hunter saw win the North American in Fairbanks. That other part of Kävik, that we know about, doesn't show on the surface. Mr. Hunter was just glad to get his dog back."

"But did you offer to buy him?" Andy persisted.

"I didn't get a chance. That dog wasn't for sale at any price."

"Where is he now?"

"Gone south aboard the *Copper Queen*. They've been gone about four hours."

"Mr. Hunter was very nice about it," Andy's mother said. "He wanted to pay the doctor bill, and offered us $200 for his keep. But we wouldn't accept it because we'd all enjoyed Kävik."

"He should have been nice," Andy said bitterly. "You could have come and got me so I could have said goodbye to him."

"I thought it was better for both of you this way," his mother said. "It would have been awfully hard on Kävik to be taken away with you standing there. Anyway, you knew this could happen. You've always known it."

"I thought maybe we could keep him when Mr. Hunter understood how he was. I—I counted on it."

"I counted on it too," his father said thoughtfully. "But how do you show a man when he refuses to be shown? When he won't look?"

"It's disappointing, but it's not a tragedy," Andy's mother said practically. "We had Kävik for a while and we all loved and enjoyed him. Mr. Hunter likes him and will give him a fine home and the best of care. That's the way we have to look at it. Now, come and eat your dinner before it gets cold."

Andy shook his head. "I'm not hungry," he mumbled.

"There's no sense being a child about this," his father said sharply. "Come and eat."

84

"Let him go," Laura said quietly. "Let him go."

Andy went upstairs and sat on the bed and looked down at the rug where Kävik had slept every night. That rock was back in the pit of his stomach again. This time he felt it would never leave.

# chapter 7

GEORGE C. HUNTER HAD BUILT A PALATIAL
home high in the hills above the city. Far below lay the pattern of the streets that led toward the concrete canyons of
the city's core. The canyons pointed toward the bay where
the commerce of the world came in by sea. Here hundreds of
industries and warehouses lined the half-moon shore, and
miles of docks reached into the bay. Some docks were lined
with great ships from foreign ports. Others, called fishermen's wharves, were packed solid with fishing crafts of all
kinds and sizes, idled here for the coming winter. Beyond
the bay lay the distant blue line of the open sea. It was to
this home George C. Hunter brought Kävik.

The first day he proudly led the dog through the big hall
into the immense living room. "Look, Edna," he called.

"Here he is. This is Kävik. He didn't die after all. Isn't he marvelous? Isn't he some animal?"

The woman looked at Kävik. She was tall and slender. Her blue eyes were chill, and her voice was sharp and unfriendly. "So this is the great dog? George, are you out of your mind? Bringing home an animal like that. I never heard of such a thing. Get him out of this house."

"You don't understand," Hunter explained. "This is the dog that won the North American Sled Dog Derby at Fairbanks. He's part wolf, Edna. There isn't another dog like him in the country today. They don't breed these fellows anymore."

"I don't care what he is," the woman said angrily. "And I don't care what he's won. He looks like a wild animal to me. I won't have him running through this house, breaking up furniture, imported glassware and antiques, and muddying up floors."

"He's not breaking anything or muddying up anything," Hunter said stiffly.

"He will, if you take that chain off him. This is a home, George, not a museum for all the junk you drag back here from the great North. I've put up with the elephant tusk you dug up at the mine, the bows and arrows, the walrus tusks, that two-hole canoe thing, snowshoes, parkas, and the old Russian guns you found. But I will not stand for you bringing wild animals into the house."

"Animal," Hunter corrected. "There's only one. And Kävik's not wild."

"He looks wild to me," the woman insisted. "And all the rest of your collection began with one. If you want to keep this brute, you put him in that run you had built and keep him there."

87

George C. Hunter said quietly, "All right, Edna. All right."

He took Kävik back outside and put him in the wire and concrete-floored run he'd had built in the backyard.

Kävik lay in a corner of the six-by-ten enclosure day after day, big head on forepaws, yellow eyes staring out over the city and over the bay to the distant line of the sea—staring toward the North.

This was a strange and frightening world into which Kävik had been brought. The threshing umbrella of sound that hung over the city drifted up to him. From the bay came the occasional deep-throated bellow of a great ship entering or leaving the harbor. Some of the sounds were repeated all day and half the night on the road in front of the house. At regular intervals planes roared low over him, the thunder of their passing shaking the earth.

The deep silences he had known all his life were gone. There was only, at rare intervals, a little less sound. His freedom of movement was now confined to a six-by-ten-foot concrete and wire enclosure. There was no boy to meet each night, to race wildly home through the trees with him, no kitchen with its delicious odors, no family sitting about a table talking in low voices, no bedroom where he slept the night on a rug at the head of a boy's bed. The very air he breathed here was different. He missed the clean sweet smell of the tundra, the fresh, biting tang of the open sea. This air was heavy with acrid fumes from a thousand different sources. They irritated his delicate nostrils. The voice and the smell of this strange world reacted on two of his strongest senses, his hearing and his sense of smell. The same fear he had known when he'd been placed in the iron cage and shoved into the mysterious darkness of Smiley

Johnson's plane came alive within him again, and never left.

Even the people who came to see him were different. They'd stand outside his run, hold their hands behind their backs as though they expected at any moment to have one bitten off, and stare at him. "He sure is different," they'd say. "He doesn't look like he's got any dog in him. A real wolf, that's what he looks like. I'll bet he's all wolf. I'd sure hate to have those big teeth after me." Sometimes George Hunter would enter the pen and pet him just to show his friends that Kävik was tame. They'd go away talking among themselves and telling George Hunter he was foolish to keep such a vicious-looking animal around. But no one ever spoke to Kävik. Not one of the many who came to stare ever put forth a friendly hand to pet him.

Then Tom McCarty returned from the funeral of a relative, and Kävik found one friend. McCarty was a lean, tough old man with a permanent limp. His leg had been crushed in a cave-in at George Hunter's mine ten years ago. McCarty had been with Hunter ever since the little man first went north to seek his fortune working in the mine, so Hunter took him south to work around his home as a gardener and handyman.

Few knew about this side of Hunter, and he tried to hide it even from himself. "We need somebody to work around the place," he'd told his wife. "Mac can do it as well as anybody else, and he comes a lot cheaper."

Tom McCarty had his own comfortable quarters above the big double garage. He kept the cars cleaned and polished, mowed the lawn, trimmed the shrubs, weeded the flower beds, and dreamed of his younger days in the far North.

The first time Tom McCarty saw Kävik lying in a corner of the wired-in run, big head on forepaws, yellow eyes staring out over the city and the bay, his heart went out to him. In the past he had worked countless times behind such animals, in weather so cold a man could freeze to death in minutes if he stood still. He unlatched the gate, went inside, and squatted on his heels before Kävik. Unhesitatingly he reached out, scratched at the roots of the dog's ears, and said gently, "Hello, Big Fella. You and me, we're two of a kind."

Kävik's yellow eyes came back from that great distance and looked into the bright gray eyes of the old man.

"You don't belong in this cage or in this country anymore'n I do. A blind man could see that. We're outsiders, you an' me. We belong up where th' wind howls across th' tundra and th' snow flies. Where your ancestors run th' ridges and where I could walk for a month and never see a livin' soul—before I had this gimp leg, that is. Me, I got no choice but to live down here—with my gimp leg. But they took your choice away from you. So here we are." Tom McCarty reached forth a big rough hand, lifted Kävik's paw, and gravely shook it. "You're a breath of God's own country, Big Fella. I'm right glad t' meet you."

Kävik's tail thumped the concrete, and Tom McCarty smiled. "That's more like it. Let's have no more of this mopin', eh? It don't buy you a thing down here."

But as the days passed, Kävik continued to mope. He was still a big healthy looking animal, but his wolf-gray coat no longer had quite the same bright sheen; his sharp ears were down flat to his head; and his eyes were not clear and interested in all that went on.

George Hunter noticed. He stood before the enclosure,

and scowled at Kävik lying in a corner. "Mac," he called to McCarty, his voice sharp and annoyed, "what's wrong with Kävik? All he does is lie there in that corner and stare out. You know about these northern dogs. What's eating him?"

McCarty had been waiting for this. He knew just how far he dared go in crossing Hunter, and he went right up to it now. "He's homesick and he's lonesome, Mr. Hunter."

"He's been here more than a month. It's time he got over that. Anything else?"

"There's another thing that would sure help."

"What's that?"

"Get him outa that pen once in a while. He's a working dog, remember? Dogs like him are used to lots of exercise and plenty of room to run. Cooped up in a pen like that is no good for him. Exercise would do him a world of good. His appetite would improve and his coat would come back some."

"Exercise, eh." George Hunter was not one to prolong acting on a decision. "We've got two acres of ground here, and it's all fenced so he can't get away. Let him out, Mac."

"Here? Now?"

"Certainly."

McCarty opened the gate and stood aside. Kävik looked at the open gate, then up at McCarty, and walked out. He stood uncertainly looking about, not understanding this sudden freedom. McCarty waved his arm, taking in the house and two acres of yard. "Go on, Big Fella," he said. "Have at it. Mush. Mush. Eat up that trail!"

Kävik trotted off a few feet and smelled of a rhododendron bush. The soft grass beneath his feet felt good after the weeks of concrete runway. He trotted on. It was wonderful to stretch his legs again, to feel the spring in his muscles, and the softness of the earth beneath his feet. Suddenly he burst into full stride, raced through a rhododendron hedge, and came to the five-foot fence. He turned along the fence at top speed, raced around a towering fir tree, burst through a stand of shrubbery, reached the next fence corner, and turned again, following it. He was a gray-white shadow streaking through shrubbery and across flower beds, running low to the ground, bushy tail stretched out, running as his wolf ancestors had run for centuries, and with their tremendous speed. His sharp ears were forward, his mouth open, sucking in great gulps of air. He was enjoying every lunging stride. He made a complete circuit of the yard, seeming to flow over the ground. Flower stems snapped; plants ripped at his passing.

Then he heard the shrill voice of the woman, high and angry. "George! Mac! Stop him! Stop him! Get that wolf out of there! He's ruining the yard. Get him out. Get him out right now!"

McCarty hobbled to cut off the racing Kävik. "Whoa!" he shouted. "Whoa! Whoa! Big Fella." George Hunter ran from the opposite direction, trying to corner him. At McCarty's voice Kävik came to a panting stop, ears cocked forward, studying the old man. "Come here, Big Fella." McCarty snapped his fingers. "Come on. The party's over." He held out his hand, walked up to Kävik, and twisted his fingers in the thick ruff of his neck. "We're gonna get in serious trouble and lose our happy home if you bust down any more shrubbery," he said in a low soothing voice. Patting the dog, he led him back to the wire enclosure and locked him in.

"Of all the stupid things to do," the woman railed.

"Turning that brute loose in this yard. Just look what he's done. Look at it!"

"I know, Edna," Hunter soothed. "Mac'll fix it up tomorrow. I didn't realize the dog would take off this way. I won't let him out again."

"Well, I certainly hope not." The woman turned on her heel and went back into the house muttering angrily under her breath.

"I guess you'd better clean up these beds and get rid of the broken limbs tomorrow," Hunter said to McCarty. "And we can't let Kävik out again. But you're right. He needs exercise. Man, wasn't he a sight! I'll get a chain with a snap ring, and you can take him walking every day. I don't want a leather collar on him. It'd wear the hair off his neck and spoil his ruff." He looked at the dog thoughtfully. "He seems to like you, Mac. Maybe if you spent some extra time with him, besides the walking, it'd help him get over being lonesome and homesick and he'd look a little sharper. Take him up to the apartment with you or anything else you like. Just don't let him loose again," he said wryly.

Thereafter Tom McCarty took Kävik for a walk every day it didn't rain. They'd go up the hill because the street ended within two blocks, and that was about as far as McCarty could walk without resting. McCarty would sit on a log, stretch his bad leg before him, and look out at the bay below and the distant sea. Kävik would sit beside him, yellow eyes searching far beyond the bay and the sea—looking always toward the north. Tom McCarty would pat the big head, and say: "You might as well forget it, Big Fella. It's a long long way by boat or plane, farther than you could ever go. So quit breakin' your heart over somethin' that can never be." Kävik listened to the old man's gentle voice, cocking his head first one way, then the other. At the end he placed a paw on McCarty's knee, where the man patted it. McCarty lifted the paw and shook it gravely. "It does no good to tell you this," he said. "But believe me, I know."

When it rained, McCarty took Kävik to his quarters above the garage. There he'd take the chain off and let him run free. On his first inspection Kävik's delicate nose sniffed out the parka hanging in the closet. The parka had been made by an Eskimo woman, and even now a faint aroma clung to it that pricked Kävik's nostrils. He thrust his nose against the thick fur, and woofed loudly.

"You know what that is, eh?" McCarty took out the parka, slipped into it, and stood before the mirror. "I brought this parkey down with me ten years ago. Wore it just once. We had a little old inch or two of snow, and I slipped it on and went outside. Everybody looked at me like I was some kind of freak. I've never worn it since." He studied his reflection critically. "Was twenty pounds heavier then, and trail hard." He sighed and took off the parka. "Know what you need down here in winter?" he asked. "Rubber boots, a rain slicker, and a sou'wester hat. Now, ain't that a fine outfit for th' likes of you and me?"

Winter came, but not as Kävik had known winter. It was drizzling rain that lasted for days, with the sun peeking through for a few hours at odd intervals.

During one of these sunny days George Hunter decided that he would take Kävik for his walk. "I want him to get more used to me," he explained to Tom McCarty. "I'm going to make a speech on Alaska soon, and show my slides. I bought some of Kävik winning the North American. I want to tell 'em about him. Then I want him there so people can see him in the flesh. That ought to give them a thrill, eh, Mac?"

"It sure ought to, Mr. Hunter," McCarty agreed.

A few minutes later Hunter strode out of the yard with Kävik on the chain, trotting dutifully at his heels.

McCarty spent the time Hunter and Kävik were gone cleaning up around the pen and the yard. He was still at this when Hunter returned, walking fast. The little man's face was stormy, and his thin lips were pressed tightly together. Kävik trotted obediently at his heels, head down, plumed tail drooping. Hunter went straight to the enclosure, shoved Kävik inside, unsnapped the chain from his neck, and slammed the door. He whirled on McCarty, black eyes snapping, his voice cutting. "Did you know about him?"

"Know what?"

"That he's the biggest coward on earth. That a good-sized chipmunk can run him to death?"

McCarty glanced at Kävik. "I don't believe it."

"Listen, Mac," Hunter was savagely angry. "You know that long white house at the end of the block? Well, they've got a dog there. As we went past, he came tearing out, barking his head off."

"What kind of a dog?" McCarty asked.

"How should I know. Just a dog, a little more than half as big as Kävik, I'd guess. Well, I thought Kävik would eat him alive. He could have, Mac. But did he? Oh, no," he said bitterly. "He almost tore the chain out of my hands trying to get away. When he couldn't he tried to hide behind me. He actually lay down on the sidewalk, Mac.

Can you feature that? A man finally came out and called the dog off." Hunter shook his head. "That great big tough-looking wolf lying there on the sidewalk, whimpering. It was humiliating, Mac. Humiliating. You never ran into that with him?"

"We always went the other way. Up to the end of the street. There's no dogs up there." McCarty glanced at Kävik lying in a corner of the cage and looking as if he knew he'd disgraced himself and Hunter. "I just can't believe it."

"I can," Hunter said. "I saw it. And Kurt Evans at the cannery tried to tell me how he was, but I wouldn't believe him. Kurt said the beating he took in the plane wreck knocked all the courage out of him. Well, something did." Hunter scowled at Kävik. "I paid $2,000 for that dog, and he's not worth a plugged nickel. Two weeks from now he's the star attraction when I show those slides and make that speech at the club. How can I show a thing like that? Why, I'd be a laughingstock."

"No, you won't," McCarty said. "Nobody needs to know. There won't be any other dogs there to scare him. You wouldn't have known today, if you hadn't run into another dog that showed fight. Let him sit up there with you and take his bows. They'll never guess."

Hunter considered that possibility. "It could work, at that. You could hold him outside until I'm ready for him; then I'll take him in. He won't have to be in the room more than ten or fifteen minutes while I make my little speech about him and everybody gets a good look at him. Yeah, it'll work." Hunter's voice turned tough, "Then I'm getting rid of him—quick."

"But he's still a nice dog," McCarty pointed out. "He looks like a big part-wolf sled dog. He makes a good show, and that's what you want him for, isn't it?"

Hunter shook his head. "Sooner or later somebody'll find out what he's like; then I'll feel like a fool. He's a cripple, Mac. A mental cripple. That's lots worse than if he had only three legs. You can feel sorry for a three-legged dog because there's nothing he can do about it. But a coward, Mac," he said bitterly, "who feels sorry for a coward? Especially a big, tough-looking one like him. There's no excuse for being a coward. None at all. Look at him, big and strong and beautiful, and he grovels and whines. I won't have it. It's $2,000 down the drain. But he goes. That's final. I'd call off the show if I could. But you get him brushed up and looking as good as possible for the club members. I don't even want to see him again."

Tom McCarty prepared Kävik for the night of what he called "Hunter's One-Man Show." The day of the show he took Kävik to his quarters above the garage to groom him. After finishing, he stood back and studied the dog. "You look fine, Big Fella," he said. "Big and strong, with plenty of good beef on your frame. Hard muscles, big chest, fine posture. You look like th' lead dog that won th' North American, all right. Nobody'd ever guess." He took the dog's big head in his hands, and said: "I've got an idea what happened to you, and I understand. He don't. I'd like to keep you around, Big Fella, but Mr. Hunter won't have it. He's a mighty proud man and he's got himself out on a limb with all his big talk about you."

Kävik twisted his head, listening to the sound of McCarty's gentle voice. He put his paw on the old man's knee, and McCarty smiled and shook it again. "You're gettin' pretty good at that," he said. "Well, let's go. You'll knock these city lads dead tonight."

Mr. Hunter's club was small and exclusive. It was situated in a grove of big trees well back in the hills above the city. Tom McCarty held Kävik in an outer room while the banquet was in progress and George Hunter showed his slides. Then Hunter came out and said, "All right, Mac, we're ready for the vicious brute." He took the chain from McCarty's hand. "You might as well wait in the car. I won't keep him long."

He led Kävik into the roomful of people and up on a small platform. There he removed the chain and ordered the dog to sit. Kävik sat on his tail, yellow eyes narrowed, and looked out over the sea of faces. George Hunter began to talk, telling about Kävik and his life in the North, his bloodlines, part wolf and malamute. He told about the North American Sled Dog Derby and what it took to be a good lead dog and how important he was to winning a race.

The room was warm. The air was heavy and oppressive with tobacco smoke. Kävik began to pant. He turned his head. There was a window near the platform. His sharp ears shot forward; his yellow eyes opened wide and his big jaws snapped shut. He rose to his feet, his whole body tense. Throughout the room people began nudging each other and smiling and whispering: "Look, he's posing! Putting on a real show, just as if he knew George is talking about him. What a ham actor!"

Kävik was not putting on a show. It was a bright moonlight night, and through the window he could see the massive bulk of mountains rising against the pale sky.

Flowing down those mountain slopes like a loose cape thrown over them was a forest. It looked wild and primitive. It looked like the mountains of his far northern home.

Tonight there was no chain to hold him back. He didn't hear George Hunter's sharp, "Down, Kävik! Sit, sit, I say!" He took two quick steps, muscles bunched, and launched his hundred pounds through the air. He struck the window and burst through with a tremendous crash of breaking glass and startled shouts.

Kävik landed on the soft earth amid a shower of glass, gathered himself, and streaked into the protection of the bushes beside the building. He heard doors slam as people rushed outside; voices called. He heard George Hunter's angry voice, and belly-crawled to the opposite side of the brush, and sneaked away. He came to a high stone wall and turned, following it, hunting a way out. Men searching came close, beating through the shrubbery, calling, "Here, Kävik. Here, boy. Come, Kävik. Come on."

He made a running leap at the wall and fell back feet short of the top. Another party of searchers came near, and he began to run in fear. It was bright moonlight, and he dared not show himself. He took advantage of every shrub, rosebush, and tree to keep hidden. He was slinking now in typical wolf fashion, trying to avoid detection. He was a gray shadow crouching behind a tree until a man beat past. He was a faint whisper of sound as he slipped through a rhododendron hedge on another man's heels. He was part of the rock itself as he crouched in the deep shadow of a boulder as a party went by, calling and beating the shrubbery. Finally he crept through a laurel hedge and edged his way along in its shadows. He was heading for the big front gate.

The gate was closed. A group of men led by George Hunter came threshing toward him. The rock wall on either side closed in to form a narrow opening to the gate. He was trapped.

Tom McCarty got out of the car parked nearby, hobbled forward, and looked down at Kävik crouched in the shadows of the laurel hedge. He looked up at the approaching men, and called: "Mr. Hunter, you'd better check that wall out back. There's a lot of brush for him to hide out in there, and the wall's pretty low. He might be able to jump it."

"All right, Mac," Hunter answered. "We'll check the shrubbery and the wall right away. You keep an eye out here." The search party turned away.

McCarty watched them leave, then said softly to Kävik: "All right, Big Fella, they're gone. You can come out now." He bent and snapped his fingers, and coaxed, "Come on. This's old Mac. You know me."

Kävik rose stealthily and crept to him. McCarty squatted on his heels before the dog and scratched his ears and patted his big head. "So, ya didn't like 'em in there and decided to leave in a hurry: Fact is, you don't like it down here no more'n I do. But you're doin' somethin' about it, and I can't. I know where ya wanta go. But it's farther than you'll ever get. It's more than two thousand miles of water and mountains and snow and ice and rivers and Lord knows what else. No dog on earth could cover that distance. I'd talk you out of it, if I could. But I know you'll try. You'll wind up someplace, maybe even dead. That would be better for the likes of you than staying here."

Kävik cocked his head and studied the old man's face and listened to the gentle words he could not understand.

But he did understand the voice and its notes of sadness and longing. He put a paw on McCarty's knee, and the man lifted the paw and gravely shook it. "You know a lot. An awful lot. We had some mighty fine talks, didn't we? You let an old man dream about his past, and you were gentleman enough to listen and not interrupt. I thank you for that. But it's over now." He glanced up, listening. "They'll be comin' back soon. You'd better be on your way." He rose and swung the gate open. He waved his hand outside. "There it is, what you've been waitin' for and wantin' since th' day you got here. It's all yours now. Go get it, Big Fella. Mush! Mush! Eat up that trail."

Kävik walked through the gate. Outside, he stopped and looked back. "Goodbye," the old man called softly, "and good luck."

Tom McCarty closed the gate carefully and stood looking at the spot of thick brush beside the road where the wolf-gray form had vanished. Then he sighed, and hobbled back to the car.

# chapter 8

KÄVIK DID NOT KEEP TO THE ROAD. HE traveled swiftly through the brush and timber, for here he was more at home and he was well hidden. He did not head back for George Hunter's palatial home, nor did he cut up the mountain into the heavy growth of timber. He was headed north. That sixth sense of direction told him the way to go.

He traveled near the road for some distance; then it began turning and twisting. He left it and cut through thick brush straight down the hill. He came in time to a network of paved streets and sidewalks with row on row of homes. Still heading north, he crossed some streets, traveled a block or two on others, then left them to cut across vacant lots and lawns. He came to a spot where he was looking down a steep street directly into one of the deep canyons of the city. The street was brilliantly lighted, and great lighted buildings punched deep into the night sky. This was the origin of the sounds he'd been hearing for weeks. Now the noise boiled up the long hill and washed over him in a continuous wave.

Kävik sat on his tail and looked down the street. He was afraid to enter that seething mass of sound and light. But there was the way to go.

He slunk warily down the street. The noise kept coming up to him in increasing volume. He stopped uncertainly many times. Once he turned back. Then the desire that had never left him since the day he'd been put aboard the boat in Copper City drove him forward again.

So Kävik came into the heart of the big city. As he trotted fearfully along he kept swinging his head, watching for something to rush down upon him, to pounce upon him, or fall and crush him. People turned and stared, startled to find such an unleashed animal trotting among them so intently. Several spoke to him uncertainly. Some were startled by his wolflike appearance and size; but before they could react he had disappeared in the crowd.

Surprisingly, Kävik was halfway through the worst of the traffic, following the course he knew he must keep, before he finally came to grief. He knew nothing of traffic lights. When he reached a corner where the crowd was thickest and seemed to be waiting, he threaded his way among the legs to the curb. He had learned something about traffic in the past hour. He waited until he saw an opening between the speeding cars, then dashed across the street. He had almost made the opposite side when a horn blasted almost on top of him, brakes screamed, and an automobile bore down upon him. A blow smashed into his side and hurled him through the air to land in a heap on the sidewalk among a forest of legs. He staggered dizzily to his feet.

People had moved back quickly, and he found himself in a small cleared space. A man in a blue uniform stood in front of him.

The man said, "What're you doing down here without a leash?" and lunged for Kävik. Had he reached slowly or said, "Come here, boy," he'd have caught the dog. But at the sudden movement Kävik leaped away instinctively, and dodged through the circle of people with the man plunging after him. Suddenly two men appeared as though to block his path. He veered. The double doors of a store yawned open before him. He dashed through and found himself in a huge, brightly lighted interior with rows of counters and a scattering of people moving leisurely about.

A small boy smiled at him. "A dog!" he said. "Here, doggie. Look, a doggie!" He pulled at his mother's skirt.

The woman turned. Kävik stood panting with fright, yellow eyes sprung wide, searching wildly for a way out. The woman grabbed her child and began to scream.

Kävik dashed up an aisle as the uniformed policeman entered the store to search for him. He streaked past several women examining sweaters, past a group milling about another counter, and came to the end of the aisle. There he confronted a man who spread his arms to trap him.

But the man hesitated. He stared at the dog, shaking his head. Then he dropped his arms and backed hurriedly away. He backed into a counter piled high with shirts, and

*Kävik raced over the man and through an open door beyond.*

104

went over backward. The counter collapsed with a crash. Kävik raced over the man and through an open door beyond. He found himself in a dark alley lighted by a single bulb. The alley was cluttered with piles of empty cartons and one large garbage can. He raced to the end of the alley and was confronted by a concrete wall. He turned. The uniformed man and another entered the mouth of the alley. Kävik flattened himself behind the garbage can, and waited.

A flashlight beam cut into the darkness and picked up the pile of empty cartons at the far end against the concrete wall. The two men advanced cautiously, guns drawn. Kävik gathered himself. When they came even with him, he exploded from behind the garbage can and dashed between their legs. So sudden was his action, he was out of the alley and back inside the lighted store before they could turn around to pursue him.

He dashed down the same aisle he'd been in before. The man who'd fallen into the shirt counter was helping a clerk gather up the shirts when Kävik rushed past. The man let out a startled, "There he is! There!"

But Kävik was gone, back out the same door he'd entered. He was again on the street where he'd been hit by the car. He turned in the direction he'd originally been following, and raced away. So swift was his flight, and so startling his appearance, that pedestrians hardly had time to gasp, "Look! Look there! What sort of animal was that? A dog? It couldn't be!"

Kävik raced down the brightly lighted street until it curved in the wrong direction. He darted across, was narrowly missed by several cars, and entered another. Soon he was leaving the lighted streets, the big crowds of people, and the open stores. The streets became dimly lit, empty of traffic and people. All the buildings were dark and closed. The city racket became muffled by distance and intervening buildings. Panic left him, and he dropped back to a steady trot that ate up the blocks.

Much later he rounded the corner of a darkened building, and there before him lay a flat body of water. A narrow dock stretched out into the water for an amazing distance. Hundreds of boats of all sizes and descriptions lined both sides of the dock. For the first time in months the wild and wonderful salt tang of the sea was in his nostrils. He heard the sleepy complaint of a nearby gull, the faint creakings of boat fenders rubbing against the dock. The dock lay in darkness except for a light at the shore end. Here the boiling sounds of the busy city were a faint echo. He did not know this was the dock on which he'd landed when he'd been brought from the North. He knew only that it was familiar and that something inside him had led him to this spot.

Kävik trotted confidently out along the dock, looking at each dark, quiet boat. He came to one and a faint but remembered aroma touched his delicate nostrils. The boat lay close to the dock. Since the tide was in, the deck was only a couple of feet below him. He leaped lightly aboard and began sniffing about. He covered the boat from end to end and picked up other familiar scents. He'd been on this boat before. But now it was dark and deserted. He whined and scratched at the door for several minutes. Finally, disappointed, he jumped back on the dock and headed out to the end—still traveling north.

Kävik came to the end of the dock, and halted. The bay stretched outward in the darkness before him farther than his eyes could see. He searched for some nearby land that he might swim to, something that would take him in the direction he was traveling. There was none. But somewhere across that water was a house overlooking the sea, with the tundra rising gently behind it. In that house were warmth and love and the companionship of people. There was a boy, at the head of whose bed he'd slept and for whom he'd waited in the dark fringe of trees each day so they could race home together. It was the boy's gentle hands and understanding voice he missed most. It was to the boy he'd given the only love he'd ever known. It was to that boy and that house he was returning. He had come as far as he could. So here he would wait, for what or for how long he didn't know.

Kävik lay down, his big head on forepaws, and looked out over the water. He lay there the rest of the night.

With the coming of dawn, Kävik rose stiffly and searched the outreaching water again. He had his long look, then turned and trotted down the dock to the boat. The tide was out now. It was too far down to jump to the deck. But he could see there was no one about.

Kävik went on down the dock to the shore side. He didn't know where to go from here or what to do. He was standing looking about when several men approached, laughing and talking. Remembering his experience of last night, he turned and trotted around a near corner. He found a dark passageway between two buildings, and went in, looking for a place to hide. An old covered stairway ran diagonally up the side of one building. Far back under the stairway he found a hole-like depression, and crouched in it. The men passed the opening without looking in.

Kävik remained in this hiding place all day. He heard the distant sounds as the city awoke and the activity around the dock increased. But in comparison to the city itself, it was quiet here. Now and then people went by. There was an occasional coming or going of a boat. Nearby a seiner was being repaired. There was the constant sound of hammering and sawing. From time to time a car would arrive or depart. Trucks made irregular appearances.

Kävik lay in the hole under the stairs, and napped and waited out the day. Late that afternoon it began to rain, but beneath the covered stairway he was dry.

With darkness, Kävik again ventured forth. He was thirsty and ravenously hungry. He found rainwater collected in an old pail on the dock, and slaked his thirst. But he did not know where to turn for food. He was standing there uncertainly when his nostrils picked up a faint, familiar scent. Saliva began to run in his mouth, and he licked his lips hungrily. It was the same scent he'd known in that kitchen in the North so far away. It was food cooking. He turned and followed the scent unerringly. It led him a block away from the dock to a small restaurant. He looked through lighted windows and saw people sitting on stools, eating. He watched for several minutes, nose twitching hungrily, licking his lips in anticipation. But he knew of no way to get the food. No one was going to come out with a bowlful and set it before him.

He was about to trot on when a pair of dogs slipped along the side of the building toward the back. A few seconds later there was a crash, then another.

A man's voice shouted angrily, "Get out of here. Get!" The two dogs raced around a corner of the building and down the street. A man in a white apron ran out and hurled a stick after them. He went grumbling toward the back again.

A woman's voice called, "What did they do this time?"

"Knocked over the garbage cans and scattered the stuff all over," the man said angrily. "I'll pick it up when I've got more time." He disappeared inside, grumbling, "The city'd better take care of these stray mutts."

Kävik looked after the fleeing dogs, then in the direction the man had disappeared. The aroma of food coming from there was very strong. Those dogs had been hungry, too, and had been searching for something to eat. He crept toward the back. The scent of food became stronger and stronger. He found two tipped-over garbage cans, their contents strewn about. He could see the man through the window, working at a stove. Kävik studied the man and the garbage cans. The cans lay in deep shadows. By detouring around the pool of light thrown by the window, he could reach them. He lay flat on his belly and, keeping in the shadows, edged across the concrete. Among a clutter of paper plates, napkins, and other restaurant discards he found cold potatoes, halves of doughnuts, wedges of pie, and other pastries and chunks of sandwiches. Under the very nose of the restaurant cook he ate his fill, then crept silently away.

Kävik had learned how to survive on the docks. In succeeding nights he added to his store of knowledge. There were other restaurants scattered for more than a mile along the waterfront, and late at night he would visit them. The other stray dogs found their food in the same manner. But they were awkward and clumsy. They'd rush in and jump at the garbage cans and send them crashing over, then grab what they could find, and dash away. Their noise brought men storming out to chase them, and more often than not they went hungry.

Kävik used stealth. He was deadly quiet. He'd been raised in the wild. He'd learned to sneak up on an unsuspecting ptarmigan, rabbit, or parka squirrel, taking advantage of every grass clump, bush, or rock for cover. The wolf in him made him particularly good at this silent approach. He kept to the deep shadows and was a slinking shadow within a shadow. He never dashed in, but crept to the back of buildings where he had learned the kitchen and garbage cans were located. He'd lie with a patience born of the wild, and wait hours for the proper time. He didn't lunge against the cans. He'd rear his front feet against them and ease them over. More often than not the resulting sound was lost in other sounds. He seldom went hungry. But his shining wolf-gray coat became dull with grime, and a long streak of tar matted the hair on one side where he'd rubbed against a fresh-coated piling.

All day Kävik would spend sleeping in the hole under the stairway where he went undetected. At night he crept forth. He came to know the docks and every building on them. He knew every other dog in the area, and there were many strays. They ran in two's and three's, or small packs of half a dozen, and they made life miserable for the restaurant people. Kävik kept to himself. The restaurant people never saw him. Even the other dogs caught only an occasional glimpse as he disappeared around a corner or slunk briefly through a shadow. He seldom trotted in the open, even at night. He was clever and furtive and swift of foot.

But every night, rain or fog or wind, he trotted the full length of the first dock he'd visited, and stood at the end, looking out over the dark stretch of water—looking to the north—still waiting. Only at that time would Kävik seem to be unaware of his surroundings and forget to peer furtively about. He'd stand straight and tall, head up, sharp ears pricked forward, eyes searching farther than eyes could see, ears straining for sounds that never came.

It was here one night that he first saw the woman. A fishing boat had been moored within a few feet of the end of the dock for days. He was looking out over the bay when the woman's voice came to him, kind and soft, "Hello, there! You're late tonight."

Kävik turned his head and looked at her. The woman sat motionless on the low, stepped-down section of the deckhouse. She wore a slicker and sou'wester hat pulled low over white hair. "Are you lost?" she asked. "Or are you waiting for somebody special? I've seen you every night. You're not like the other mutts. They're here because they've got no other place to go. You're here for a reason. I can tell."

Kävik's sharp ears came forward, and he listened to the gentle voice. "You have the class and dignity of a gentleman. You look well fed, too, not half starved like some of these others. But you're just as dirty. I'd like to give you a bath and cut that tar off you. You're not a local dog. I've seen your kind before—in the North. Did you come down on a boat and get lost somehow? Are you waiting for your boat to come back?"

Kävik continued to watch her as long as she talked to him. When she stopped, he turned and trotted back down the dock.

The woman sat on the low deckhouse every night, waiting for him. She talked to him, and he'd prick his ears forward, and listen. He liked her voice. Soon he came to look for her. One night she had something for him to eat. She came ashore, put the plate on the edge of the dock, and returned to the boat. "There you are," she said. "It's what we had left over from dinner."

The food was on a white plate, almost like the bowl he'd had in the North. He advanced and smelled the food. Then he began to eat. Thereafter the woman had some tidbit for him almost every night. She'd always put the dish on the dock and return aboard the boat. Then Kävik would advance and eat.

Quite often a big, sturdy-looking man in a short oilskin coat, sou'wester hat, and knee-high boots sat beside the woman. He'd blow clouds of smoke from a foul-smelling pipe and listen impassively while the woman chattered.

"He's such a nice dog. Don't you think he's a nice dog, John?" the woman would ask.

John would remove his pipe, and say, deliberating, "Seems to be."

"He comes out to the end of the dock every night," the woman said. "I'll bet he's looking or waiting for someone."

"Maybe he just likes to look at the bay," John said. "I've seen animals go to certain spots and stand and look for no apparent reason."

"He has a reason. Haven't you noticed how sad he looks, John?"

John laughed and blew a cloud of smoke. "Every stray looks sad, Martha. Don't let your sympathies run away with you."

"He isn't a stray," Martha insisted stoutly. "He belongs

to someone. He's quite a noble dog. He really is. Just watch him, John."

John shook his head. "You're always getting all wrapped up in a lost cause or a lost cat or some kind of cripple. Use your head for once. If he's so noble what's he doing down here?"

"I don't know. I wish I did. Such a dog running loose." Martha clucked her tongue disapprovingly.

"Don't let it bother you," John said. "The dogcatchers will be coming one of these days to clean out these strays. The restaurant people are complaining."

A closed panel truck appeared one day and parked near Kävik's hideout under the stairway. Two men got out. One carried a short length of rope and the other a large net. Kävik heard the clamor of dogs coming from within the closed truck.

From then on, Kävik saw the panel truck often. Dogs he'd seen almost every day began to disappear. It became much easier to get food, for now there were fewer dogs to tip over the garbage cans.

Then one night, as he stood on the end of the dock, looking off across the bay, the two men came up behind him. When he became aware of their stealthy steps and turned, they were surprisingly close.

Both men stopped. The one carrying the net said in a friendly voice, "Nice doggie. Here, boy. Come on, boy." He advanced slowly, cautiously, making the net ready.

The second man began uncoiling the rope.

The one with the net said, "Here, boy. Come, boy. Easy, boy."

Kävik didn't like the man's voice or the way they advanced with bent-kneed stealth. The dock narrowed at this point, and he could not dodge past them. Behind him was the bay. He looked down at the boat where the man and woman sat each night. In two quick jumps he landed on deck and raced its length.

Then he was trapped tighter than ever. They came at him, one on either side of the cabin, and the deck where they walked was just wide enough for their feet. The man with the rope had picked up a length of pipe for a weapon. The net man dropped the net because the space was too narrow to use it. He snatched the pike pole off the cabin roof.

Kävik crouched against the low rail, yellow eyes narrowed. His lips rose, exposing the long, cruel teeth. A growl rumbled in his throat.

The cabin door opened, and the woman and the man stepped on deck. "What are you men doing here?" Martha demanded. "This is a private boat."

"Sorry, lady," the one with the pipe answered. "We've got to get this dog."

Martha looked at the crouching Kävik, and said, "Oh, it's him. Look, John. He's come aboard."

"I see he has," John said, and studied the two men.

"Keep back, lady!" the pike-pole man said. "This animal's dangerous."

"What are you going to do?" Martha demanded.

"We've got to get this dog," the pike-pole man said.

"With an iron pipe and a pike pole?"

"If necessary. He's vicious."

"Nonsense," Martha said. "Put down that pike pole and pipe. Give me your rope. I'll get him for you."

"I wouldn't try that, Martha," John said.

"Lady, if you'll just get out of the way," the pike-pole man said, "we'll have him in a minute. Then we'll go."

"Give me the rope." Martha held out her hand.

"He'll bite, lady. I'm telling you."

"Martha, let the men take care of this," John said. "They know the dog."

"They don't know this one." Martha still held out her hand. "But I do. I've watched him and talked to him for days. Will you give me that rope! And put down that pipe and pike pole. They belong on this boat."

The man handed her the rope without another word, and laid the pipe on the deck. His partner put the pike pole back on top of the cabin. "You're takin' an awful chance, lady," he said.

Martha took the rope and went toward Kävik, talking quietly. "Come now," she said. "There's no need to show those teeth at me. You know me too well for that."

Kävik stopped growling, and the snarl disappeared. His ears came forward and he watched the woman. Martha bent over him and stroked his head and said: "That's a good boy. I knew you weren't mean. What a silly thing for anybody to think about you." She slipped the rope about his neck, and said, "All right. Come on, now. Come."

Kävik rose and followed the gentle pull of the lead. Martha led him to the man with the net, and handed him the rope. "Here's your dog."

"Not mine," the man said. "We're roundin' up these strays for th' city pound."

"You're the dogcatchers?"

"What else?" The man held up the net.

"I—I didn't know," Martha stammered. "I didn't see the net."

"Well, thanks for catchin' 'im." The men turned to leave.

"Wait," Martha said. "What—What will they do with him?"

"Keep 'im a while," the net man said. "Then if nobody claims him, they'll—" He looked at Martha's face and changed what he was about to say to, "They'll put 'im to sleep."

"Oh!" Martha said. "Can anyone take him?"

"Sure. Buy his license and he's yours."

"We'll take him," she said quickly. "You can leave him here." She held out a hand for the rope.

The man shook his head. "I can't do that. My job's to catch 'im. You come down to th' pound, and they'll take care of it there." He nodded at his partner. "Let's go."

Martha and John Kent watched the men leave, with Kävik trotting dutifully at the net man's heels.

Martha said, "I caught him for them. I gave him to them."

"You couldn't help it," John said. "They were bound to get him. You saved the dog a beating, I'm sure."

"I didn't think," Martha said miserably. "I didn't see any net. I thought they owned him." She looked at John, eyes pleading. "We can have him, John. They said we could. All we have to do is pay for his license. That's only a couple of dollars. Oh, John, let's get him."

"We can't, Martha," John Kent said kindly. "You know we can't."

"Why can't we? We had Tippy until he died."

"Tippy weighed about twelve pounds. This dog is six or seven times bigger. Stop and think. This is a thirty-two-foot boat. There's no place for a dog that size."

"But they'll kill him. And he's such a nice dog."

John Kent put a big arm around her. "I know," he said kindly. "But you can't save 'em all, hon. You saved Tippy, and before him, Buttons. But they were little. Not like this fellow. He'll take up as much room as two men. Maybe somebody will come and get him. He'd be great on a farm or some big place."

Martha Kent shook her head. "Nobody will take him, I know," she said positively. "They'll do away with him." She sat on the stepped-down roof of the deckhouse and gripped her hands tightly together. "I watched him every evening," she said. "He'd come trotting out to the end of the dock and stand there like a statue and look out over the water. He was looking far away. Looking toward some place I couldn't even guess at. And he was so sad when he stood there. He trusted me, and I caught him and gave him to them. I betrayed him, John."

# chapter 9

JOHN KENT LAY QUIETLY SO HE WOULD NOT
disturb Martha. He stared up at the night-blackened ceiling.
Through the open port he heard the small stirrings of the
night. Water gurgled around the base of the pilings; feet
thumped on top of the dock. A disturbed gull complained
sleepily. Martha had been terribly upset over the dog. He
realized now how much she had wanted him. All that feeding and talking to him every night had been part of her
scheme to get him aboard gradually so she could keep him.
She was not only sneaking up on the dog's blind side, he
thought, but mine, too. He thought she was asleep, and then
her troubled voice said into the darkness, "John, how long
will they keep him before they put him away?"

"A week, maybe two," John Kent said. "They give a dog

every chance to be adopted. Somebody'll take him sure—a dog like that."

"I hope so."

Silence settled again in the compartment. He thought Martha had drowsed off, when she said: "I wonder if they'll give him a bath. He was awfully dirty, and he had that big black streak of tar."

"Sure they will. They'll want him to look good for any prospective takers."

"I hope so," Martha said again. She was silent for some time, then, "John, how do they—dispose of them?"

"Electricity or gas or some such. One thing I know. It's quick and painless."

"He was such a nice dog."

It was much later when John Kent knew she had fallen into a troubled sleep.

But there was no sleep for him. The evening's happenings and Martha's taking it so hard had knocked all thought of sleep out of him. He felt sorry for the dog. But then he felt sorry for any lost animal. He was especially sorry for Martha. She was a gentle person and she had great compassion for all animals.

Life aboard a salmon troller hadn't been easy for Martha. She didn't particularly care for the sea and fishing. When she first came aboard, Martha had sewed and read and done embroidery to pass the weeks of waiting. For four years he'd had the terrier, Tippy, to keep her company. Tippy died, and this past year Martha's eyes had failed some. She was forced to give up sewing, embroidery, and reading. Now she spent hours listening to the radio and playing solitaire. She needed another pet to fuss over and worry about. And she wanted the big wolflike dog.

John Kent argued with himself against the big dog, and his arguments were sound. But finally he ran out of objections, and lay there staring through the port at the outside night and the bull's-eye patch of sky. When at last it began to turn gray, he eased himself out of the bunk, dressed quietly, and tiptoed outside. He climbed to the dock and struck off toward the city.

At eight o'clock that morning John Kent was at the city pound, talking with an attendant. "Two of your men picked up a dog on fishermen's dock last night. He's a big fellow, gray coat with a streak of tar on one side. Looks like an Alaskan husky."

"Back here," the attendant said, and led John Kent to a wire pen that held several dozen strays. Kävik lay in a corner alone, big head on forepaws.

"That's the one," John Kent said. "Has anybody called about him or anything?"

"Nobody ever calls about the strays we pick up on the docks."

"I was told I could have him by buying a license." John Kent held out a bill. "Do you have a rope of some kind?"

An hour later a cab drew up at the shore end of the dock, and John Kent got out, leading Kävik. "Well, here you are again," he said to the dog. "This time you're legitimate." They went down the dock and aboard the *North Star*.

Martha took one look at Kävik, and her face broke into a happy smile. "I knew it!" she said. "When I woke up and you were gone, I guessed."

"How could you?"

"When you've been married to someone forty years, you know." Martha bent, took the rope off Kävik, and stroked his big head. "I prayed all morning that you'd still be at the pound when John got there," she said. "Am I glad to see you again! I played a mean trick on you last night when I gave you to those men. But now it doesn't matter." She dug her fingers into his thick coat and looked at him critically. "You've been eating pretty well, but not as good as you will from now on. And you need a bath. You're awfully dirty. We'll have to cut that tar out of your fur. But first we'll all have breakfast."

The small galley was like the kitchen of the home he'd known in the North. The same delicious aromas of cooking food assailed his nostrils. There were the familiar rattling of pots and pans and the clatter of tableware, as Martha hurried about the galley, setting the table. He had his own bowl in the corner of the galley and he ate the same food Martha and John Kent ate. From time to time Martha held out tempting morsels, which he lifted delicately from her fingers, his yellow eyes fastened unwaveringly on her face. He felt at home with these people.

"You see," Martha said happily, feeding him a strip of bacon. "He's used to this sort of treatment. He's not just another dock stray."

"I guess you're right," John agreed.

After breakfast Martha got out the galvanized tub and placed it in the middle of the galley. Giving him a bath took both people. He was a big dog and he filled the tub. He stood quietly while John poured water from a huge dipper over him, and Martha lathered him from nose to the tip of his tail. She kept up a stream of chatter while she worked. "My, but you are dirty! I'll bet you haven't had a good bath in months. Stand real still and I won't get soap in your eyes. You're a gentleman. You know that?"

The bath took some time. When it was over, they

rubbed him down with old towels. Then Martha settled down to brushing and combing. She cut away the long black streak of tar from his side.

"Look, John," she said, working away industriously at a gray coat that was now several shades lighter. "Isn't he about the most beautiful dog you've ever seen?"

"He's quite a dog." John smiled. "What're you going to call him?"

Martha considered, plying the brush vigorously, "We can't call him Bobby or Tip or Skippy or any ordinary name like that. It's got to be a special name that means him."

"How about Misty or Dawn? He's got that gray sort of color that goes with both."

Martha shook her head. "They don't mean him. John, does he look like any breed you know about?"

John Kent shook his head. "No one breed. But I have seen dogs in the North that resemble him. I'd bet he's got some wolf in him. It's in the shape of his head and in his eyes. Especially in the eyes. I've seen wolves trot just like he does. Not slinking, not really trotting. But sort of gliding over the ground. I've got a hunch about this fellow."

"What's that?" Martha asked.

"Years ago, when the dog sled was the chief mode of travel in the North, the Indians and Eskimos often bred their dogs to wolves so they'd get a tougher, smarter, and stronger animal. But since the airplane has come into being and is so much faster, dogs are now bred principally for the sport of sled-dog racing, very little for work. To find one this size and with his looks is unusual. My guess is that he's a 'throwback' to a wolf ancestor, and not far removed. The dog in him could be malamute, Siberian husky or McKenzie River husky. In all likelihood he was born in the

North and brought down here. If he's not acquainted with a dog sled in some manner, he should be."

"He might have escaped from some sled-dog kennel around here."

John shook his head. "This fellow's a valuable animal. If a kennel had lost him, they'd have immediately contacted the pound. They told me nobody had asked about him."

Martha laid down the brush and sat back on the floor. She smiled at Kävik. "There!" she said. "Now you're beautiful." She frowned. "We don't really know much about him, except that he's been living on the docks with the rest of the strays, and he doesn't belong here. He's used to being cared for. He probably didn't come from around here. He's a northern dog, a kind they don't breed anymore. Yet here he is."

"It doesn't make sense." John leaned forward, hands on knees, and scowled at Kävik. "Mister, you're quite a mystery."

"That's what we'll call him," Martha said.

"What?"

"Mister Mystery. It means him."

"Mighty odd name." John Kent filled his pipe and lit it. "Fits him, though. Mister Mystery."

"He has to have a collar," Martha said. "A big studded collar."

"I'll get it the first time I go to town."

Martha had little time left for the radio, and none at all for cards. Kävik got his collar, a glistening leather circlet studded with iron heads. He'd never worn a collar, but he soon became used to it. Martha combed and brushed him daily until his coat shone with the same wonderful gloss it had had in the North. She took him for daily walks on the leash, but she did not go far nor was she gone long. She avoided stores and restaurants where she might meet people. She kept to the back streets and deserted docks. She was determined no one should see Kävik and claim him. In the love these two people showed him, Kävik might have been expected to forget and become happy with his new home. But he did not forget.

He did not stand on the dock every evening and stare across the water now because Martha purposely did not take him up there. But when five o'clock came he knew.

At five o'clock each night he scratched at the door, and whined. Then he paced to the window and reared his forepaws against the frame to look out. Night after night he kept it up, until finally Martha sighed, put the rope on him, and led him to the stern of the *North Star*. There he stood, ears pricked forward, and looked across the water. Martha let him stand for a few minutes; then she said: "All right, you've had your look. Let's go back. It's getting cold." He followed dutifully, and dropped into a corner of the galley and rested his head on his paws.

"I was hoping he'd forget whatever it is that takes him out there," Martha said.

"Give him time. We've only had him a few days. He'll come around."

"I hope so," Martha said. "You know, there's something about the *Copper Queen* that attracts him, too. Every time we go by, he wants to go aboard. Do you suppose she means anything to him?"

"I doubt it. The *Copper Queen* belongs to George C. Hunter. If he'd lost Mister Mystery he'd have turned the city upside down looking for him. But take Mister Mystery

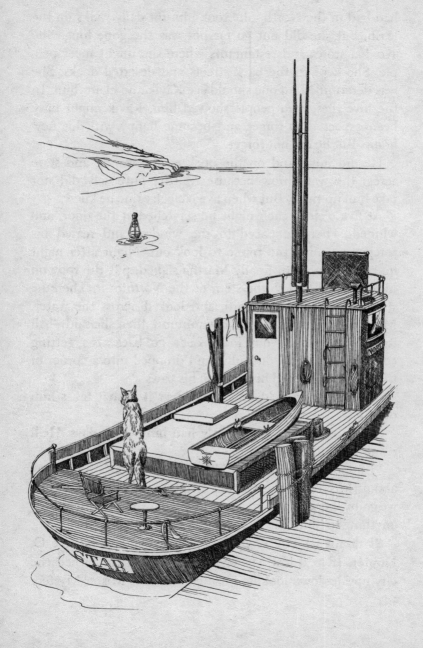

aboard the boat and let him smell around and see what he does."

"I've been afraid to," Martha confessed.

"Stop worrying about him. And you don't have to put a rope on him every time you take him out for a minute. He's not going to run away."

"You put the rope on him when you take him out the last thing at night."

"Habit," John Kent said. "Just habit."

"Of course." Martha smiled down at Kävik. "Remember, you said he'd be in the way all the time because he was so big? Well, he's not. He moves so gracefully and quick. He seems to know where I'm going to be next."

"You're a hopeless romantic." John smiled.

The next day Martha took Kävik aboard the *Copper Queen*. He sniffed all about while she followed, holding firmly to the rope. In the passing weeks the winter rains and winds had wiped out all traces of familiar scent. There was nothing here to interest him anymore.

After that, he scarcely paid any attention to the *Copper Queen*. This pleased Martha, and she told John about it. "I do believe he's forgetting and is going to accept us," she said.

"Did you doubt it?"

"Yes," she said seriously. "He still stands and looks off across the bay every night, you know."

"Martha," John said patiently, "that doesn't mean a thing. Animals are creatures of habit, even more than

*There he stood, ears pricked forward, and looked across the water.*

people are. Why, I've known of brown bears who return to the same spot on a stream to fish year after year. A wolf will pass a half-dozen high spots of ground and climb the same slope to sing night after night. A coyote will do the same thing. An eagle will pick one snag out of a forest of snags and light on it every day as long as he lives. Habit, Martha. Mister Mystery trotted out on the dock one night and looked at the bay. Now he wants to do it every night. I don't know why. But I do know, it's habit. Now will you stop worrying about it?"

"Well," Martha said, "maybe you're right."

"Of course I am. We'll be starting back north in a couple of weeks. Then there'll be no bay for Mister Mystery to look over each night. The change of scenery and locale will probably break this habit."

So the next two weeks passed. They loaded the galley shelves with grub, filled the gas tanks, and one morning eased away from the dock. Martha and Kävik were in the wheelhouse with John when he swung the bow north and headed out across the bay toward the distant sea. For the first time in five years Martha was happy to see the city's skyline fade from sight. With it went the nagging fear that any hour someone might come along the dock searching for Mister Mystery.

Kävik suddenly reared front paws against the wheelhouse window and looked out. His yellow eyes were sprung wide, and his lips lifted in a grin. Miraculously, he was at last crossing the impossible water.

Martha put an arm around his neck, and said, "Look, John! Mister Mystery is happy we're going."

"It gets me, too." John patted the dog's head. "Even

after all these years. Every season is like beginning a new adventure."

Day after day they plowed north at a steady nine knots. The cities and towns bordering the coast became smaller, until they were no more than villages. There were great stretches of open beach and sometimes stands of timber came down to the water's edge. The silence Kävik had known all his life was there once again.

This was not the country he remembered, but he was traveling steadily in the direction he knew he must go, and the restlessness increased within him. He paced about the deck, the galley, and the wheelhouse all day. His black nose sampled the sea breezes, and reached for scents that were not there. His sharp ears were pricked forward, listening. When they came near the coastline or stopped somewhere to gas up, his eyes were constantly searching.

"Why can't you relax?" Martha said one night, and closed the galley door to keep him in. "You've had a big supper. Come here and let me brush you." He obeyed because he always did, but Martha could feel the restlessness in his big body as she worked over him. "You said he'd get over that habit of standing and looking every night," she said unhappily to John. "But he hasn't. Now he paces around all day long. It seems, the farther we go, the more discontented he becomes."

"Not discontented," John said. "Restless. The first time you came north it was all strange to you, too. Remember? You were trying to see and experience everything at once. It could be the same with him. We think he's from the North. But we don't know for sure. Maybe he's never been aboard a boat before or seen country like this. He can't reason, so he has to experience everything by hearing, seeing, and smelling. This could be a completely new world to him, and he's finding it exciting and thrilling. Also, don't forget, you used to walk him on the dock every day for exercise. He hasn't had a walk since we left. He's been cooped up here for days, like an animal in a cage. He's going to pace like a caged animal."

"Perhaps you're right. I don't know," Martha said stroking Kävik's glistening coat.

The evening of the tenth day they came in from out at sea and entered a tiny, sheltered cove. The cove had been punched into the side of a mountain that crowded to the edge of the beach. There were a small dock far back in the cove, an oil-storage tank, and a caretaker's house. They tied to the dock, and John went ashore to hunt up the attendant. He returned in a few minutes and said: "Nobody here. A sign on the door says he'll be back in the morning. We'll lay the night here and gas up tomorrow."

Martha prepared supper, and after they'd eaten, Kävik began pacing again, from the door to the window and back to the door again. Martha stood it for a few minutes, then reached for her coat and the lead rope. "All right, we'll go for a walk on the dock. I guess it does get pretty tiresome for a dog cooped up aboard all the time." She put the rope on Kävik, and the three of them went out and climbed to the dock.

The day was ending, and the shadow of the mountain lay across the dock and the small cove. Biting cold flowed down off the mountain slope. Martha pulled her coat tight, and they walked about the dock looking at the cove and the mountain. Finally Martha sat on a piling end, holding the rope loosely in her hand. John Kent stood beside her, hands buried in his pockets as he looked about, smiling. This was the big land he loved. Kävik stood in front of them. His ears were erect, his nose tilted slightly as he reached hard for some scent. Martha said, "Mister Mystery, if I just knew what you were looking for I'd get it, so you could relax and be happy with us."

Kävik paid no attention to her voice. He was reaching, feeling, smelling, hearing with that animal sensitivity no human possesses. He had no way of knowing that once again he stood in Alaska. He knew only that the very breeze funneling down off the high mountain beckoned to him, heavy with the remembered tang of spruce and hemlock forests. The chill bite of snowfields was laced with the faintly musty scent of deep, sunless canyons. The great forest hung a black mantle over the mountain and swept down to within a hundred feet of the dock. Up there, among the trees, he could see the edge of the white cover of snow. Silence hung over the mountain, and in it he heard the soft whisper of wind through the trees. All these sights, smells, and sounds were old friends with whom he'd spent his whole life. They reached for him now, holding forth a promise that nothing else could.

Kävik looked to the north, as he had for months. For the first time there was no impassable water. He was looking across land. Up there, through those trees and across the mountain, was the way to go. Somewhere beyond waited the boy and the only life he knew and wanted. Somewhere out there was home.

He trotted forward so quickly that before Martha could tighten her fingers around the rope it had slipped through her hand.

Martha jumped up and called, "Mister Mystery, come

back. Come back, Mister Mystery." The dog trotted to the edge of the dock and off. She called again in a commanding voice, "Mister Mystery, you come back here! Come back! Do you hear me?"

Her tone of voice stopped him. He turned his big head and looked at the two people. The look he gave them was as impersonal as if he'd never seen them before. Then he trotted on purposefully toward the beckoning trees and the snowline.

John shouted angrily, "Whoa! Mystery. Whoa, boy!" That sled-dog command stopped him as abruptly as if someone had grabbed the end of his trailing rope. So well had he been trained as a lead dog by Charlie One Eye, that he didn't move as John Kent started across the dock toward him.

Martha's low voice said, "Let him go, John. Come back."

"He just wants to wander around," John began.

"No," Martha said. "He knows where he's going. Let him go, John. Please."

"You know what you're saying?"

"I know. Let him go."

John Kent turned and waved his arm at the waiting Kävik. "Go on, beat it. Mush! Mush!" He walked back to Martha, and asked, "Why'd you do it? Why'd you want to let him go, Martha, after all these weeks?"

"He's got someplace special in mind," Martha said, watching the dog with sick eyes. "I thought so when he used to stand on the end of the dock and then on the stern of the boat and look across the bay. Then when he became so restless as we headed north, I knew. I've watched it grow on him day by day."

John Kent turned and watched Kävik go straight up the

slope, enter the trees, and disappear without a backward glance. "You were right all along," he said. "How could I have been so blind?"

"He wasn't happy with us one minute," Martha murmured. "He never could have been, with whatever it is driving him so. He was just a passenger on board. He went along until he found the spot where he wanted to get off. I couldn't keep anything as sad and unhappy as he was."

The last light went out of the sky, and night came down in chill, thickening layers. Martha drew her coat closer and began to shiver.

"Come back aboard the boat," John said gently. "You're getting cold."

In the galley John lighted the fire, and soon heat spread through the small compartment. He sat down across the table from Martha, packed and lighted his old pipe, and began blowing clouds of smoke.

"I wonder where he's heading," Martha said.

"It could be anywhere farther north. I guess that makes him a bigger mystery than ever."

"Yes." Martha looked around the galley. "It seems so empty now."

John put the pipe away. He reached across the table and patted her hand. "We'll get another dog. Any kind you like."

"A little one," Martha said. "Mister Mystery was big."

"We'll get a pup so we'll know all about him," John said.

"I'd like that. A puppy."

"No more mysteries."

"No more mysteries," Martha said. Then she put her head down and quietly began to cry.

# chapter 10

KÄVIK ENTERED THE DARK FRINGE OF TREES
and climbed steadily until he came to the snowline. Here
he stopped and stood, nose lifted, as if he quested the
breeze, seeking direction. Then he struck out without hesitation, going straight north, going home to the boy.

Animals have always possessed this homing sense of
direction. It leads wild geese, ducks, swans, and a host of
smaller birds winging across thousands of miles of trackless
plains and tundra, vast mountain ranges, and amazing ex-
panses of water to remembered lakes and streams and
valleys far in the Arctic where they nest and reproduce in
summer. In the fall they fly the same miles back again. It is
that homing instinct that leads the salmon halfway around
the world to spawn and die in the very stream, the very

spot where years before they were born. Man knows this to be true with animals, yet with all his knowledge he can neither do this himself nor explain it.

Kävik knew nothing of maps and of great distances. He could not know that facing him was four hundred miles of some of the roughest land to travel over in North America. The mountain range he was heading into had many nine-thousand-foot peaks, and a few were as high as fifteen thousand feet.

He could not know that the area he was entering contained more glaciers for its size than any other in the world. There were countless frozen streams that the spring breakup would turn to raging, icy torrents. There were mighty canyons whose depths the sun never plumbed, great stretches of barren tundra buried deep under winter snow, and dense forests where roving packs of timber wolves were king. Had Kävik known and understood these hazards, it would have made no difference. He was going home, and now there was nothing to stop him. Nothing but the trailing rope that he snagged within the first mile. There was a knot in the end to keep it from unraveling, and this wedged between two stones and held him fast.

He sat down and surveyed the situation. Then he calmly twisted his head, got the rope in his jaws, and with one snap bit it in two. That left only a foot of it dangling from the collar, which did not hinder him. He trotted on, going deeper into the timber.

It was good to breathe the sharp, clean air, to feel the snow under his feet again, and piling against his chest. In a clear spot where it lay smooth and fluffy, he stopped and rolled in sheer delight. Then he rose, shook himself, and went on.

Kävik traveled all night under brilliant stars and a full moon that made weird patterns of the birch and hemlock trees. He crossed the face of the mountain, followed the backbone of a barren rocky ridge, and finally dropped down the opposite side. Near dawn he came out on a high, sharp point. Below him lay a great expanse of snow-covered tundra that stretched away to the black mass of a range of mountains. The tundra was thinly dotted with small clumps of willows and groves of scrub trees. A keener wind cut across this flat land. Pausing to rest, Kävik stood head up, ears pricked forward, reaching for whatever sound or scent the utter silence and the wind might bring. There was nothing but the stars and the moon flooding the earth with winter night's soft light. He was starting down to the flat tundra plain when he heard a sound. It began on a low note. As it rose higher and higher, other voices joined in, until it was a whole chorus filling the night. Wild and beautiful it beat against the mountain slopes behind him and flowed down to spread across the tundra plain below. Then it died slowly away, only to begin again and rise and swell as other voices joined in. A whole pack, or family, of wolves was congregated somewhere on a hill and was singing its high, wild song to the beauty of the night.

Kävik listened, his whole body tense and waiting, searching for one special call. His own voice swelled, ready to answer. But the call did not come. Finally he dropped his head, trotted down the slope out onto the tundra plain, and headed toward the distant bulk of the mountains. The song of the wolves followed him for a long time.

Here on the flat, open land the going was harder. Wind had drifted the snow into great ridges, and he had to detour

around, floundering chest deep. Dawn found him ravenously hungry, and beginning to tire. Hunger now became
uppermost in his mind. He began watching for small animals. There were a few fresh tracks here in the open. For
the most part, animals kept to the timber where there was
food. Finally he came to a fresh rabbit track with small
doglike prints running beside it. The tracks eventually dived
into a tangle of willows that had been laid almost flat by
the weight of snow, and there Kävik left them. He circled
the willows and picked up the tracks again. Not a hundred
yards beyond the willows he came onto a red fox crouched
in the snow over the fresh-killed body of a snowshoe rabbit.

Kävik stopped. Fox and dog studied each other. The fox
lifted his lips in a warning snarl, but Kävik paid no attention. His eyes were on the rabbit, and the thick, warm
smell of blood was in his nostrils. He licked his lips and
started forward. The fox snarled again. Suddenly he
snatched up the rabbit and bolted away at top speed. Kävik
leaped after him.

The fox was not so fast as the dog, and he was further
hampered by the weight of the rabbit. They charged
through a thicket, across a cleared space, and into a dense
growth of scrub trees. The fox dodged about among the
trees, trying to shake Kävik. But Kävik gained steadily.
They burst out of the trees, and the fox started straight
across a wide open space to the next brush patch. Halfway
across, he dropped the rabbit and raced on at top speed.

Kävik stopped at the rabbit, dropped into the snow, and
began to eat.

The rabbit was small, and it had been many hours since
Kävik had last eaten in the galley aboard the Kents' boat.

The rabbit did not satisfy his hunger, but the sharp edge was gone. Now as he trotted on he began searching for a place to rest.

He found a small hole in the snow against a steep bank. A few seconds of digging uncovered the opening to a cave. He started in, then stopped as a rank odor filled his nostrils. This was the winter den of a sleeping bear. He backed out hurriedly.

A brittle sun burst from behind the distant mountains and flooded the earth with cold sunlight. Finally Kävik entered a stand of timber and found an upended tree. There was a hollowed-out depression at the base of the roots. He crept in, turned around several times, lay down with a tired sigh, and curled into a tight ball.

It was still light when Kävik awoke. After a good stretch and a test of the chill breeze with his delicate nose, he began plowing through the snow again—heading north. He was ravenously hungry, and on the lookout for food. The distant mountains gradually drew nearer. The brush patches increased in number, and the tree groves became larger. The flat land gave way to rolling hills and brush-choked ravines. Signs of game became more numerous, and it was not long before he jumped a snowshoe rabbit and tore through the snow after it. Like a white wraith the rabbit, with its big furred feet, skipped lightly over the snow ahead of him. But Kävik broke through at every lunging stride. Soon he began to tire, and the rabbit pulled easily away from him and vanished into a thick patch of brush. He raised several others before dark, but each time he gave up after a short chase when the rabbit began to leave him.

The moon and stars came out, and once again it was

almost as light as day. The night's cold clamped down with biting intensity, and the earth became utterly still.

Kävik entered the mountain range through a narrow valley that led back into a mighty nest of jagged peaks. He followed the valley until it took a turn. Then he went up over the ridge, across a barren stretch of land, and finally dropped into a second timbered valley. In a cleared spot, he came on a small band of moose that had yarded up to escape the deep snow. Here was food aplenty. Kävik chose a young animal, and dashed toward the herd, barking wildly, trying to stampede it. The leader was a huge bull with great palmated antlers branching to many needle-sharp points. He turned to meet Kävik with lowered head and huge splayed hooves that with one savage blow could stamp the life out of the dog. Kävik danced around him, trying to lead him off so he could get at the half-grown calf. When the moose charged with a bellow of rage, Kävik coyly led him away by keeping just out of reach of the dangerous antlers and hooves. But when the dog turned suddenly to double back to the herd, three young bulls were waiting, and bore down upon him. He tried the maneuver again and again, driven by hunger to taking desperate chances. Finally he tried to dodge between the protecting young bulls. He misjudged the quickness of the big animals, and a sweeping horn caught him and flipped him into the air with a startled yelp of pain and surprise. He fell into a tangle of willows, and scrambled up just in time to dodge a pair of striking hooves that would have split his skull open. He ducked about among the striking feet, then turned tail and ran limping down the valley floor. The moose did not follow, and he soon fell back to plowing steadily on through the soft snow. His side ached and burned where a sharp horn had raked him, and for some time he limped badly. But as the night wore on, the limp and the ache disappeared. He was following the course of a small stream that was now a dead, twisted smoothness under the snow. He kept to the valley floor all night, and for some reason there was no game. His hunger pangs continued to grow.

Full day had burst, cold and bright, from behind the peaks when he came out of the trees at the upper end of the valley and faced a cluster of a half-dozen log cabins. Smoke billowed from each cabin. The surrounding snow was cut and trampled. He had come onto the Aurora Mine. It was shut down for the winter, but the few families who worked it during the summer remained the year round. The men spent the winter months hunting and trapping.

Kävik's nose led him unerringly between the houses and out to the garbage dump. There he found frozen chunks of bread, bones of caribou and moose, along with a variety of other frozen table scraps. He began bolting down the food. A door opened, and a woman started from one of the cabins, carrying a pail. He gave her only a glance, and continued eating.

The woman saw him, and stopped. She began to scream, "Phil! Phil! A wolf! A wolf!"

A man dashed out of the house, caught up an ax, and charged at Kävik. Kävik recognized this danger, grabbed for a caribou bone, and turned to flee, but too late. The man hurled the ax. The flat of the spinning blade smashed against the side of his head, and sent him sprawling. For a moment he lay unable to move while the man bore down upon him. Other doors burst open, disgorging men who snatched up weapons and ran toward him. Then he wobbled uncertainly to his feet and ran for the trees. Sticks and hand axes rained about him.

Kävik ran a good mile at top speed. Then he crawled up beside a log, and lay down. His head throbbed and he still felt dizzy. Blood dripped steadily into the snow from the gash the ax blade had made. The blood soon froze on his face, but the pain remained. He lay close to the log, head on forepaws, eyes closed, and waited for the pain to pass. Sometime later he became aware of a steady sound, and raised his head above the log. Two men were following his trail. Behind the protection of the log he crawled to the nearest trees, then rose abruptly to run. Coming to the edge of the trees, he saw that he'd have to cross an open space to the next clump in full view of the men. He heard their shouts as he lunged into the open. Then thunderous explosions rocked the morning. Puffs of snow geysered up on either side of him. One burst almost under his nose, showering him. Though the snow puffs and the explosions followed him all the way in his wild dash for the trees, surprisingly he was not hit. Then he charged into their cover.

Kävik fled down the valley, up a steep slope, and out into a flat area of timber. Sheer exhaustion finally ended his panicky flight. He stopped on a high point and looked back over his trail. There was no sign of the men, so he dropped flat in the snow, and rested. The pain in his head had subsided to a steady ache. He licked his paw and rubbed it over the wound, but it didn't help. If he could only reach it with his tongue to cleanse it. He lay there until he was completely rested, then went on at a much slower pace.

He was still hungry and on the lookout for food. It came unexpectedly. A ruffed grouse that had plunged deep into the soft snow to sleep during the cold was startled awake at the sound of the dog's feet. Kävik leaped, struck with his paw, and knocked it out of the air. Before the grouse could gather itself again, the dog's teeth closed on its back.

The grouse satisfied his hunger and sent new strength coursing through his tired muscles. He went on, moving steadily deeper into the fastness of the mountains. The snow at this higher elevation was lighter, making travel easier.

The day spent itself, and the night closed down. The stars and moon came out. Once again it was almost as bright as day. Kävik stopped on a hillside to rest, and keened the dead silence for what it might bring. He heard the call begin, and his head came up. His whole body became tense with expectation. The sound swelled and swelled until it filled the night and there was no telling from which direction it came. The wolves were singing again.

Kävik listened intently as he had before, searching each voice, waiting for one special note. It did not come. When it was over, he started to move on. Then a new call brought him up short. It began so softly it seemed a part of the night, and he was not sure just when his keen ears first heard it. In the stillness it rose slowly, soaring to a high, clear call of sadness and longing. It faded away into the massive blackness of the mountains. A deathlike hush; then it began again, rising to the same high soulful cry and dying away. This was the note he'd been listening for. He'd heard it many times as a pup. As he grew older, it had taken on meaning.

Somewhere out there a wolf was singing, pouring her loneliness and longing into the night, calling for love, calling for a mate. It was the most natural thing in the world for Kävik to sit on his haunches, tilt his big nose toward the stars, and send forth his own far-reaching cry.

As his voice died away, the answer came, rising high and clear, riding over valleys and mountains to hang trembling on the still night air.

Kävik went plunging headlong down the slope. He stopped once and called again, and again the answer came back, much closer now. He charged on through the snow at top speed, and came, finally, to a tiny clearing nestling at the foot of towering mountains. There, waiting in the black fringe of trees, he found her.

He paused at the edge of the clearing. He could see her sitting in the snow in the deep shadows across from him. He advanced cautiously into the open, and stopped uncertainly. The wolf moved as carefully from the darkness of the timber, and sat down. The two regarded each other.

She was younger than Kävik. She was slim and strong and alert. Her color was dark gray, and in the moonlight he could see that her fur was soft and sleek. Kävik crossed the little clearing and sniffed noses with her. The next moment she was leaping about him with all the friskiness of a puppy. She raced around the little clearing, dashed at him and nipped him, then spun away. Kävik leaped after her, his manner every bit as puppyish as hers. Finally she streaked into the dark trees, coyly leading him a mad chase. Kävik stayed at her flying heels as they circled about through the trees and returned again to the clearing. They were sniffing noses, tails waving happily, when the female suddenly lifted her head, and her ears shot forward.

Kävik looked. There across the glade, standing at the edge of the tree shadows, watching them, was another wolf.

He too had answered the female's call for a mate. Now he advanced slowly into the clearing, head down, watching Kävik. He went straight to the female, and they sniffed noses. Then the female turned, trotted off a few feet, and sat down, leaving Kävik and the male wolf facing each other.

This new wolf was almost as big as Kävik, and several years older. His coat was thick and coarse and almost black. He stood stiff-legged, head lowered. His manner said plainly he meant to fight for the favor of the sleek female.

Kävik's first impulse was to run away, as he'd run from the dogs in Copper City, and as he'd tried to run the day Mr. Hunter walked him down the block near his home. But the sight of the sleek young female sitting on her haunches, lips lifted in a grin as she looked at first one, then the other of them, held him in a grip as strong as life itself. Except for the short time he'd been with the boy, most of Kävik's life had been spent in harness, training for a race or staked to a ten-foot chain. The spirit of the mating season had touched him only briefly, and from afar. Tonight, for the first time, it was near, and so powerful it overwhelmed all fear and reason.

As he watched the wolf approach, ears laid back, lips beginning to lift, Kävik knew what was coming. He and the black wolf must fight to the death for the favor of the young female. And she, remaining completely aloof, would go with the victor. The wolf in Kävik accepted this, but the domestic dog in him, bent to man's will for thousands of years, hesitated. It was almost his undoing.

*Then the female turned, trotted off a few feet, and sat down, leaving Kävik and the male facing each other.*

The attack came so suddenly it bowled Kävik completely off his feet, and the wolf's teeth were at his throat. The battle might have ended there, but as the wolf struck for the throat, his teeth clamped down on Kävik's studded collar instead. The next instant, Kävik reared up with a snarl of rage and threw the wolf off. Then he was fighting with a savagery he had never known before.

The wolf was an experienced fighter. He knew all the tricks: the speed of attack and wiles of retreat; how to defend, and how to feint and strike and get away. And his incentive to win was as great as Kävik's.

Kävik was bigger and stronger. But he was not so quick, and he had never fought a wolf before. The dogs he had met were slow and plodding, in comparison to this wolf. Again and again he tried to close with the wolf and sink his teeth in the soft flesh of his throat. But whenever Kävik struck, he was always met by the wolf's clashing fangs. Soon both their mouths and lips were cut and bleeding. No matter how he tried, Kävik could not penetrate the wolf's lightning-quick guard. He enveloped the wolf in a whirlwind of rushes as he tried to hurl his greater weight against the animal to bowl him over and so expose his throat. But the wolf always avoided him, danced away, then back to slash the dog's shoulders and neck and the side of his face with razor-sharp teeth.

The wolf remained almost untouched, while Kävik's blood streamed from numerous cuts. He was beginning to tire badly. All this time the female sat on her haunches at the edge of the timber, and smiled. This was not tragedy to her, but fulfillment. It was the way of life and love in the wild.

As Kävik tired and began to pant hard, the wolf took to

146

rushing. He kept the dog turning and twisting wildly to protect his feet and throat from those slashing fangs. Once those teeth closed on a leg or reached his throat, Kävik knew he would be finished.

But Kävik possessed a quality the wolf did not. He could fight in ways other than pure instinct. As the lead dog for a sled team he had been taught to think, to reason. In a burst of enthusiasm Charlie One Eye had once admitted: "When th' race starts it's all Kävik's. I just run along to encourage 'em." And it was true. As the leader, Kävik had been responsible for keeping the team strung out and working hard. He set the pace. He'd had to know when to swing wide to clear an obstacle that could wreck the sled, or avoid rotting ice that would break through and plunge them to their deaths. He'd had to be ever alert for trouble on the trail, and ready to adjust quickly to any emergency. He was adjusting now from force of habit.

In his desperation he no longer fought with wolfish instinct. He was fighting with his head. He rushed, jaws low to the snow, and at the last instant swept in to snap at the wolf's front legs. Twice he did this, and each time the wolf danced aside. The third time he rushed, feinted low, and as the wolf leaped aside, Kävik whirled on his hind legs and lunged after him so quickly he caught the wolf just as he struck the ground with all four feet bunched. For the first time Kävik's driving shoulder smashed into the lighter animal and threw him back on his haunches. Then Kävik was on him, and his big jaws found the throat. The wolf fought madly to free himself, but it was useless. Kävik was merciless. He bore the wolf to the ground. His teeth drove deep for the jugular, and found it.

He held on for several minutes, even after the wolf had

ceased to struggle. Finally he let go and looked across his fallen foe to the female. She still sat in the snow, watching. His head came up; his sharp ears shot forward, and he looked at her with steady yellow eyes. He had the dignity of a king and the bearing of a champion. Once again he was a throwback to an arctic wolf father. He was Kävik, the wolf dog.

Kävik stalked across to the female, and they sniffed noses. She licked the wounds on his face and neck. Then she trotted into the darkness of the timber, where she stopped and looked back, waiting for him.

Kävik hesitated. This was not the direction he wanted to go. The female returned to him. She licked his face again, and whined pleadingly. Once more she trotted into the timber, and stopped to wait. Kävik followed to the edge of the trees, and halted. He turned his head to the north and stood utterly still, as if listening for some far-off sound. The female whined again, and he looked back at her. The desire that had driven him to answer her call and to fight to the death for her was all-consuming.

Kävik went to her, and she touched his face gently with her muzzle. They trotted into the gloom together, traveling not north now—but due east. He was answering the age-old call of his kind. With the female at his side, Kävik ran through the vastness of the land and the magic of the night.

# chapter 11

KÄVIK AND THE FEMALE RAN THROUGH THE deep blackness of the timber and the intermittent moonlight. The speed of their travel was geared to his slow pace. The battle with the black wolf had not only sapped his strength; his injuries were painful, and he'd lost a great deal of blood. His head, where the ax blade had landed, was swollen and feverish. The black wolf had torn that wound open further. Sometime during the fight the remaining foot of rope had been chewed away. Only the studded collar remained. The female ran close at his side, giving him the comfort of her presence. But finally he could go no farther. He crawled into the protection of a patch of brush, and lay down. He was panting and trembling with fatigue, and every injury he'd sustained was on fire.

The female lay beside him, and began to lick his wounds. Kävik relaxed with a tired sigh and let her minister to him. In time he fell asleep, and his last sensation was of her soft tongue cleansing his feverish head wound.

When he awoke it was daylight, and the female still lay beside him, head up, watching. She turned and touched the wound on his head gently, and whined. They stayed there most of the day while Kävik rested and the female continued to cleanse his wounds.

The sun dropped behind the massive peaks, and night spread its shadows over the land. The night wind came up with a biting edge, and the temperature fell many degrees. A rising moon painted bright silver patches on the snow and deepened the dark under the trees. Kävik rose stiffly, stretched, and scented the crisp air with his nose for whatever messages it carried. He was ready to travel.

For the first few hours their pace was little more than a good trot. The female ran close at his shoulder, her warm muzzle touching his neck often in encouragement. Gradually stiff, bruised muscles loosened, and at last Kävik was again running with most of his swift, gliding stride. They fled through the night like silent gray ghosts, noses close to the snow, hunting their first meal together.

Late that night they raised their first rabbit, and the female taught Kävik the wolf's trick of chasing a rabbit in relays until they caught it. He had never shared his food with any animal. As a sled dog he'd bolted his food quickly before some other dog could rob him. Now he and the female devoured the rabbit together, growling amicably. They caught two more before the night was over. While they were eating the third, Kävik again heard a single wolf singing. He listened, but had no desire to answer. With the coming of dawn they found a hole under a rock ledge, and lay down side by side to sleep the daylight hours away.

So the days passed, and they ran together through moon and starlit nights, traveling ever deeper into the primitive mountain range. Under the female's constant ministrations Kävik's many wounds healed. Even the ugly ax cut on the side of his head gave him no further trouble. He thought of the boy and the home farther north, and tried to turn the female. But she always led him away east, and he followed. She was his mate, and in the law of the wolf they would remain together as long as they lived.

The fact that wolves mate for life makes a wolf pair particularly solicitous of each other. Kävik was now living, thinking, and acting like a wolf. He had never before experienced this close companionship with any of his kind; nor had the female. She had lived her life with the pack. Like newlyweds, their affection for each other grew stronger each day. They became a good team. As they ran shoulder to shoulder hunting, they learned to act together. They were sure of each other and were happy and content in each other's company.

The female knew their existence was precarious, and wariness was a part of her life. This wariness she communicated to Kävik. When they rested, one or the other of them would occasionally rise up to look about and listen to make sure all was well.

Several times other lone wolves tried to join them. This they both resented, and they stood side by side, growling and showing their teeth. The lone wolf would always back off and turn tail.

One morning, after a successful night's hunt, they came into a small valley, and there met a half-dozen other wolves. Kävik was all for ignoring them and going on, but with a yelp of recognition the female trotted forward eagerly. Soon they stood together, tails waving, and sniffing noses like old friends. They had stumbled on the pack with which she had been raised, and they were welcoming her back.

Kävik stood a little apart, waiting for her. It may have been that which saved his life. He heard a sound, looked up, and saw the plane. It exploded over the rim of the valley like a giant red bird of prey, and dived straight at the cluster of wolves. The earth shook with its thunder, and sharp explosions came from it. Two wolves were immediately down, kicking in the snow. The others scattered in all directions, racing for the valley's edge and the protecting fringe of timber. Kävik streaked for a nearby patch of brush. As he did so, he glimpsed his mate fleeing for the timber with the red plane roaring down upon her. Little geysers of snow were spouting up about her fleeing form.

He was about to turn back and go to her when the plane banked sharply and came roaring back across the valley straight at him. He dived into the brush and flattened in the snow. It screamed low over him, banked, and came back again. It circled back and forth across the valley, searching for more wolves. But suddenly the valley was empty. Three still forms lay where they'd fallen. Finally the plane landed on the snow and skidded forward. Two men climbed out and went plowing toward the dead wolves. Their excited voices sounded strange in the silence.

Kävik crawled frantically through the brush to the far side. There, out of sight, he rose, dashed for the trees, and vanished.

From the protection of the trees Kävik watched the men

gather up the three dead wolves and return to the plane. He waited until the plane had taken off and disappeared. Then he ventured into the open and looked around for a sign of his mate. There was nothing.

Kävik circled the valley, hunting the spot for which his mate had been running. There he found several tracks leading into the timber. He could not tell which was hers.

He chose one set of tracks and began following it. After a short distance he found drops of blood on the snow. Farther on, he came to where the wolf had lain down to rest. There was a great red patch in the snow. The wolf had risen and gone on, but steady red drops marked her path. The rest stops became more frequent. A half mile farther on, he came upon her huddled close against the base of a stump, as if for protection. Kävik whined, put a paw on the soft gray coat, and pulled. The wolf rolled lifelessly away from the stump. It was not his mate, but another female that looked very much like her.

Kävik sniffed about the still form for several minutes, then left. He trotted back to the little valley where the tragedy had occurred. He found the second pair of tracks that he thought might be hers, and tried to follow them. He lost them when they merged with several others deep in the trees. He stayed with the tracks, and they led him straight away from the valley. In an hour he caught up with four wolves trotting down the bottom of a ravine. She was not among them. He retraced his trail, passed the valley, picked up their old tracks of the previous night, and followed them for several miles in the hope that she might have gone that way. But he found nothing. Then he remembered that she liked to keep to high ridges. So for several hours he ran a high, brushy ridge always on the lookout for her. He visited dense stands of timber and thick patches of brush where she might be hiding if she were wounded. Again he found nothing.

The sun dropped out of the sky, and night shadows flowed over the earth in deepening waves. The stars came out, brittle-bright, and the cold wind set the snow-laden hemlock limbs swaying. Finally Kävik sat on his haunches, a lonely figure on a barren knoll, and sent his worried cry ringing through the stillness. It was answered almost immediately, but it was not the voice he wanted to hear. He had traveled miles this day, and he was getting tired and hungry. He didn't know where else to search. He had covered practically all the land over which they'd traveled last night, and his anxiety was increasing.

He started back toward the little valley, drawn there because that was the last place they'd been together. He stopped frequently and sent his call into the night. Sometimes it was answered, and each time he listened hopefully. It was past midnight when he finally approached the valley again. He sat down on the tree-studded rim and once more poured out his heartbroken call. The answer came immediately from the opposite side, high and true and urgent.

Kävik went charging down through the trees, his weary legs driving him forward in great lunging bounds, and she came to meet him.

They met in the middle of the valley in a swirl of flying snow and happy barks and whines. There was much tail waving, anxious sniffing, and loving nips as they leaped about like frolicking pups. They had been apart all day and half the night, and were happy to be united again.

As they traveled steadily inland, the snow became deeper, and most animal life disappeared. Moose and deer traveled to other parts of the country where they could feed better and where they could not be helplessly trapped by predatory animals in belly-deep snow. Most of the small animals retired to subterranean passages under the snow, leaving the upper world to the grouse, ptarmigan and snow-shoe rabbits. In this deep snow it was easy for the rabbits to avoid the heavier Kävik and his mate, and it was next to impossible to stalk grouse and ptarmigans. So the two found lean feeding.

One night as they searched through the dense woods, Kävik suddenly halted and threw up his nose, questing the night wind. He immediately identified the scent born to him, and pushed eagerly ahead. The female followed more slowly. She halted several times, whined, and started to turn back. Each time Kävik went back to her, touched her reassuringly, and they pushed on. Finally he came to the edge of the trees and crouched in the snow. The female crept up beside him and flattened out uncertainly. They were looking into a clearing. There were dogs staked out and cabins with sleds pulled up against their walls and smoke drifting into the night air. And, most important, from the cabins came the delicious aroma of cooking food. Kävik licked his lips and wrinkled his black nose and sniffed and sniffed with remembered delight. He trembled with the desire to leap up and go charging into camp and sniff noses with the dogs, to hear the voices of people again and feel their hands caress him, to sleep near them and to eat their food.

The female moved nervously beside him and finally began backing away into the trees. Kävik tried to reassure her, but could not. He turned and reluctantly followed her. In the protection of the trees they circled the camp, and then Kävik's keen nose picked up another scent he remembered: the garbage dump. He followed it and came to the fringe of trees again. There it was, several hundred feet from the nearest house. He remembered his past experience, and this time he did not walk boldly forth. He studied the houses first, then the staked dogs, then chose the way in which he could go and not be seen. It led beside a snowdrift some three feet high, behind a pair of stumps, and the full length of a log.

Kävik stepped out, trotted quickly to the snowdrift, and crouched, waiting for the female. She hung back in the dark under the trees, and refused to follow. He returned to her, touched her reassuringly with his nose, and went back to the snowdrift and waited again. She lay down in the snow, and refused to budge.

Kävik went on then. He crept the length of the snowdrift, past the stumps. He came alongside the log. A door opened at the nearest house, light fanned across the snow, and he heard voices. A man stepped from the house and crossed to another, passing within fifty feet of the log behind which he crouched. Kävik waited until the man disappeared inside the next house; then he crept the length of the log to the garbage dump. There was food aplenty. He bolted down chunks of frozen bread. He found what had been a whole leg of venison with meat still clinging to the bone. He carried this back to the female. He returned a second time, found a deer's rib cage still intact, and carried it away.

They dragged their spoils a mile into the hills, and feasted. They hung about the camp for several days, and each day Kävik scavenged the garbage pile for food. But the female would not go near, and Kävik carried the food back to her. The sight of the dogs, of men and houses, and the human scent that permeated everything repelled her. These things lured Kävik, and kept him close.

The third day she refused to accompany him to the edge of the timber. This was too close to man for her. She had made up her mind to leave. She trotted off a way and waited for Kävik to follow. He hesitated, looking after her. Then she deliberately trotted away through the trees, and disappeared. Kävik stood, uncertain for a few seconds, then ran after her.

They went on, and the snow remained deep and the game scarce. Now the female became tired struggling through the snow, and Kävik took the lead, bulldozing a foot-deep trail with his powerful chest. The female began to grow restless, and she displayed an increased interest in holes under stumps and rocks or the caves in the edge of banks. She spent much time nosing about among them, digging the snow away and inspecting them. Kävik did not understand. At such times he good-naturedly lay down in the snow and waited for her to finish.

They were traveling in this manner one day when they came upon a small cabin in a grove of trees. They stopped and inspected the cabin from a safe distance. Though there was a rick of snow-covered stovewood near the door, there was no sign of life about. No smoke curled up from the chimney. No fresh tracks were about the cabin. Kävik was about to go on, when a wayward breeze brought a faint scent to his delicate nostrils. His head came up and he stepped forward toward the cabin, big head swinging about, his yellow eyes searching. He found what he was looking for hanging from a rope fastened to a tree limb, a haunch of caribou.

Kävik sat down under the meat. He looked up and drooled and licked his lips. Days of good eating hung there.

The female came forward cautiously. She sat down beside him, looked up at the haunch, licked her lips, and whined. She was very hungry. An occasional rabbit and a few mice and shrews dug from the deep snow had been slim fare, especially for her. Now, looking up at the meat, she forgot her natural caution and her fears of the possible nearness of man. She crouched, eyes on the haunch so invitingly near. Her body gathered, and suddenly she shot upward. Her straining jaws snapped a foot beneath the prize, and she fell back in the snow. She tried again, driving upward with all her strength, but she came no nearer. Six weeks ago she'd have made the leap, but now she was getting heavy and a little clumsy. She crouched panting, staring hungrily upward. She knew she could never make the leap.

Kävik had been watching her, and now he made his own leap upward. His big jaws snapped shut just inches short of the haunch. He crouched again, yellow eyes fixed on the meat. He gathered his legs well under him, big muscles bunched like coiled springs. He launched himself upward with a mighty leap. When his jaws clamped shut, his teeth were firmly sunk in the haunch. He hung, swinging gently back and forth, refusing to let go. His added weight was more than the thin rope could hold. It snapped, and dog and caribou haunch crashed into the snow.

Both animals were instantly after it. Crouched side by

*His big jaws snapped shut just inches short of the haunch.*

side, they tore ravenously at the frozen flesh. It had been many days since they'd enjoyed such a feast. They were not aware of anything but food until the shot tore into the silence. The female let out a startled yelp, and jumped, then fell. She was up instantly, and they both raced for the protection of the trees. The gun crashed again, and bark flew from a stump inches from Kävik's head. Then they were dodging swiftly through the trees.

They ran until the female collapsed exhausted in the snow. Kävik returned to her. She lay panting heavily, and there was a great spreading red stain on her sleek side. Kävik licked her face, and whined. He pushed at her with his nose, trying to get her to rise. But she did not move. He licked the spreading stain, found the wound, and cleansed it with his tongue. He kept watching anxiously down the trail, expecting any minute to see the man appear. After a long rest the female finally got to her feet.

Kävik once again took the lead, breaking trail for her, and they continued on. Their pace was terribly slow now. She did not go far before she stopped to rest. Kävik returned to her. The wound was bleeding again, and he licked it clean, but it continued to ooze. He rubbed against her, and whined, urging her on. In this way they moved forward for several hours, and finally began to climb a long, gentle slope toward a barren, rocky ridge. Several hundred yards short of the ridge she staggered under a ledge of overhanging rock, and lay down. No matter how he tried, Kävik could not get her up again.

Kävik lay down close beside her for a time. He licked her face gently, and cleansed the wound again. It had almost stopped bleeding. He laid his big head lightly over her neck in a protective gesture. Then he turned and crept outside and climbed to the top of the ridge where he could watch their back trail.

The man was not in sight. He waited for some time, but the man did not appear. Kävik turned and started back to the female. He jumped a snowshoe rabbit on the way. The ridge had been blown almost barren of snow by the wind, and his footing was good. He caught the rabbit within a hundred feet. He carried it back with him, crept under the ledge, and laid it in front of her. She had not moved since he'd left. She lay stretched on her side, eyes closed. Her flanks scarcely moved as she breathed. She opened her eyes briefly when she smelled the rabbit, then sighed, and closed them again.

Kävik whined and nudged the rabbit closer. He touched her neck, her face, and her closed eyes gently with his nose, whining anxiously all the while. But she did not rouse. He tore the skin from the rabbit, exposing the warm red meat. Other than a faint twitching of her nostrils, she gave no sign. He cleansed the wound again, though it had stopped bleeding. Finally he lay down close beside her and stretched his big head out flat, touching her in understanding and sympathy. He lay there and watched the daylight hours slip away. The sun disappeared. The stars came out one by one, and the northern night closed down, bringing its cold. A cutting wind swept over the barren ridge and into the valley below. It passed with a low moaning over the ledge under which Kävik and his mate lay. But it did not touch them.

For hours Kävik lay beside his mate. The untouched rabbit froze solid. He smelled of it several times, and his mouth watered. Though he had not satisfied his hunger at the cabin where the man had shot at them, he did not touch the rabbit.

Once during the night he felt her shiver violently. He licked her face and whined softly, but she did not rouse. Again he laid his head across her neck lightly, as though he would reassure and warm her. He stayed in that position for a long time. Finally he crept out and climbed to the ridge again to make sure all was well. Under the stars and a thin moon he could see their back trail clearly. He sat down to watch, and at last he saw movement against the darkness of the trees. Soon the figure of a man plodding steadily up the slope on snowshoes came into view.

Kävik slipped far down the ridge toward the man; then he deliberately stood in plain sight, etched against the sky. The man stopped, raised his gun, and fired. The echoes slapped back and forth against the hills. Kävik ducked behind a rock as the bullet snarled angrily above him into the night. He showed himself again briefly. Then he ducked over the opposite side of the ridge in an effort to lead the man away from his mate.

Kävik peeked back over the ridge a minute later, but the man was not following. He was a trapper who understood the ways of the wild. The bloodstained trail stretched ahead, leading him straight to the ledge where Kävik's mate lay. The man was following that trail.

Kävik tried once again to lead the trapper astray. But this time the man merely glanced up at him, and then went on.

Kävik rushed back along the ridge to warn his mate. She lay utterly still, as before. He whined and nudged her with his nose. He put a paw on her shoulder and scratched to rouse her. His whine turned to an urgent bark. She did not move. Her eyes did not open. He sat down on his haunches and looked at her, ears cocked forward anxiously. She looked just like the other wolf he'd found huddled against the stump after the plane had roared over them. That wolf had not moved again. He knew now that his mate was like that wolf. She would never move again, no more than would the half-skinned rabbit that lay frozen solid before her nose.

He crept to her and sniffed over her for several minutes. He cleaned the wound on her side, though it no longer bled. He touched her nose gently with his.

Finally the knowledge that the man approached claimed all his thought. He licked her face, and whined a last time. Then he crept out from under the ledge and went up the slope to the top of the ridge.

Kävik stopped there and looked back. Though he could see the ledge and the opening where she lay, her still form was hidden from view. Far down, the black shape of the man climbed steadily. Kävik felt the wind cut into him, and heard its mournful sighing through the trees. The man kept coming.

He turned, at last, and went slowly down the far side of the ridge. Once again he was going due north—alone.

# chapter 12

KÄVIK TRAVELED STEADILY ALL THAT NIGHT and the next day. He was in very low spirits. Never in his life had he felt so alone. Hunger ate at him, but he had no desire for food. He made no effort to catch the few rabbits he jumped or the grouse that exploded out of the snow under his nose. He stopped often at first and looked back, remembering his unprotected mate lying under the ledge and the approaching man. But he went on. Once he sat on a barren hill, tipped up his head, and poured his heartbreak into the the frigid silence. His cry echoed through the mountains, and died away. There was no answering call from anywhere.

But grief, like winter, cannot last forever. Soon hunger drove Kävik to hunting again as he traveled ever north. As his grief dulled, the memory of the boy and the home increased, until once again the driving urge within him was all-possessive.

The first warm breath of a Chinook blew up from the south and sliced deep into the snow pack. Almost overnight lavender crocuses, the first unmistakable harbingers of spring, pushed slender stems through the hard crust of snow and spread their blooms to a warming sun. Long before he saw it, Kävik heard running water beneath the melting snowpack.

Then, by sea and by air, the great tide of wildlife began its annual surge into the North. And Kävik was part of it. But his travels were harder. Geese, ducks, and swans flew high over the jagged mountain ranges, over glaciers and streams, mile-deep canyons and valleys. Kävik had to travel them on foot, covering many extra miles that were beset with dangers the flyers knew nothing of.

In winter the glaciers and streams were easy to travel, for they were covered with snow; but now the warm winds and longer hours of sunlight were fast melting the snowpack. In summer they present an obstacle that most men, even when especially equipped, do not care to tackle. They are huge lakes and rivers of ice hundreds of feet deep, sometimes miles wide. They snake great distances through canyons and valleys. When the snow has melted off their surfaces, they present a barrier more formidable than the land itself. Sun and running water turn the surfaces slick and sharp, and gouge out impassable crevasses and unscalable cliffs. Footing is precarious. There is the constant danger of slipping into a crevasse from which escape is impossible. The lands jammed between the glaciers are the rugged tops of mountains and mile-high ridges where traveling is equally hard and dangerous. There is little food in this area for a dog to eat.

Kävik knew none of this. The glaciers lay across his line of travel, so he must cross them. Now his forward progress was slow. At times he detoured so far to go around a barrier that it seemed he might have lost his way or forgotten the reason for his endless journey. But this was not true. Once the way was clear, he always came back on course again. He became leaner than ever from lack of food. The pads of his feet were worn down by the sharp ice ridges. The trails he left across some of these glaciers were spotted red.

Only once did he hesitate at the sight of a glacier. He came down off a high ridge and stopped on a point of rock above the immense ice pack. The timbered slopes of the far side were almost lost in misty distance. The surface of the glacier was cut and gouged with pressure ridges and a whole network of deep crevasses. Here, near the edge, was a deep crevasse he could not cross. He would go around.

He started on the long trip to circle the ice field. He had no way of knowing he would have to travel almost a hundred miles to get around it. Hour after hour he worked his way along the edge of the glacier, traveling east. Sometimes the land jutted into the glacier mass, and he thought he'd found a way around. He would go out to the very tip of the land. There he met the ice again, going on and on. He became worried. He was always traveling east when his way led north.

Finally the glacier narrowed down, and he came out at the tip of a headland and looked at the far shore. Here it was no wider than many others he had crossed. Unhesitatingly he stepped out upon it.

He came to a series of small crevasses. Some were so narrow he jumped them easily; several he detoured around. An ice slide, where huge blocks of ice lay scattered like a child's building blocks, held him up for a few minutes until he found a trail through it. He was almost across when he came to the sheer ice wall across his path. It was six to eight feet above his head, too high to try to jump. He began following along its base, looking for some sort of trail to the top.

He found a spot where a section of the wall had broken off and piled a mound of ice at the base. From the top of the mound to the top of the ice wall was no more than four feet. He climbed gingerly to the top of the mound, balanced and crouched, then leaped for the top of the wall. He got his front legs over the top, but there was no grip for his claws. He scratched frantically with his hind legs, trying to find footing, but there was none. He slipped back over the edge, and fell. One hind leg caught in a crevice. His body swung back against the face of the wall, wrenching his imprisoned leg. Then he fell onto the pile of ice and rolled to the bottom. He lay there, momentarily stunned.

When he scrambled to his feet, one hind leg hung useless. He tried to put it down, but the sudden stab of pain made him whimper. He stood for a minute balanced on three legs. Then he began hobbling along the face of the wall. A half mile farther on, the ice wall ran out to nothing, and Kävik found himself standing on top.

It was not far to hobble to the edge of the glacier and to the timberline. There he found a runoff of a small stream from the glacier, and followed it a short way until he came to a hole-like depression against the bank. He crept in and lay down. The coolness of the earth felt good. He looked himself over, but there were no open wounds to lick. There was a large lump high up on the injured hip, but it was nothing to cleanse with his tongue. He put his head on his forepaws and looked out at the day and watched the light slowly fade as night came on. A breeze blew across the glacier, cooled by the ice, and this coolness felt good.

He tried to sleep, but the pain in his leg would not let him. He lay through the night and watched the dawn sun spray light across the face of the glacier and chase the dark from under the trees. Finally he pulled himself stiffly to his feet and hobbled out. The leg had stiffened during the night, and the pain was a steady throb. He could not bear the slightest weight upon it.

Kävik hobbled to the creek, and drank long. Afterward he stood for a moment and looked to the north. Then he started painfully off on three legs. He was very hungry.

He could not travel far without resting, and his pace was a three-legged hop. It took him all day, hobbling painfully on three legs, to travel the distance he'd have made before in two hours.

He spent the night curled against the side of a log. The next morning he could still put no weight on the leg. But at dawn he was again on his way.

Though game became plentiful, he could not catch it. And the animals seemed to know. The rabbits made no great effort to dash off at his slow, painful approach. A squirrel sat up within a few feet of him and boldly scolded him, then flicked its tail disdainfully and ran up a tree. He did not know that at last he had passed the glacier area. He knew only that his one chance for food lay in finding it already dead or in stumbling on some sort of cache he could raid. He went hungry another day, and spent the night curled up beside a bush near a small stream.

With the dawn he was again traveling, moving at the same slow pace, but going north. His leg was worse. A clump of grass touching it as he passed brought a whimper of pain. The distance he could travel in a day was becoming less and less. Lack of food was sapping what little strength the injured leg had not already taken. He hobbled along, head down now, eyes sick and unseeing. Sometimes he staggered. He staggered right onto food.

He frightened a ptarmigan off her nest when he almost stepped on her. The ptarmigan fluttered about in front of him, trying to draw him away. But he just stood there, looking down at the nest of eggs under his nose. His nostrils were full of the fresh smell of the bird, and when he dropped his nose and smelled of the eggs the scent grew stronger. The eggs were warm. Automatically his tongue went out and licked an egg. Never in his life had he eaten one. But he took it in his mouth and clamped down on it. It burst, and the warm, rich yolk filled his mouth. He had learned something.

Kävik broke the next egg with a tooth, and licked up the contents. He ate every egg while the mother ptarmigan fluttered about and scolded him. He felt better after his meal.

Late in the day he was lucky again. At a small stream he frightened up a nesting duck. This time he hunted for the nest, and found it in long grass at the edge of the stream. He cleaned out the nest while the mother duck hung about, gabbling angrily and making threatening little runs at him.

That was the last food he found. But he continued on,

his progress slower now than ever before. His stops were many and long. He'd drop flat on the ground, dead-dog style, his thin flanks heaving with the effort it had taken to hobble each short distance.

At last, the good back leg gave way, and his hindquarters sank to the ground. He sat there for some time, head down. When he tried to rise by leaning forward and pulling with his front legs, the good back leg refused to hold his weight, and he fell over on his side. He lay full length, eyes closed, gathering the last of his strength for one more try. He heard the voices of a flock of crows going over. And he caught the far-off cries of gulls, riding a fresh, sharp breeze. But he was too tired for these sounds to take on meaning. He did not know that at last he had crossed the high mountains and the greatest glacier area in the world. There, before him, less than half a mile away, lay the sea.

# chapter 13

THERE WERE TWO DAYS OF SCHOOL LEFT, BUT Andy Evans was not thinking of that as he tramped through the woods on the way home. He was thinking of Kävik, as he did almost every day when he made this mile walk home. He remembered how the big dog used to wait for him here and how they went racing back down the trail together. He should stop thinking of that, he told himself. Kävik was two thousand miles away. He'd never see him again.

And so, coming home through the trees on the next to the last day of school, Andy Evans could not believe his eyes when he saw a dog standing in the trail before him. But such a dog! This dog wavered on three legs, and his ragged coat was matted and dirty. His flanks were sunken, and he was so thin Andy could count his ribs through the mat of hair. He stood with his head down, looking obliquely up at the boy. Only the general shape of the big head and the steady look from the yellow eyes were the same. The ragged, bushy tail waved slightly in recognition.

For a moment Andy hesitated, blinking his eyes. Part of his mind said he was really seeing Kävik, and another part rejected the idea as impossible. This was not Kävik. This was a specter.

Then Andy dropped his books, and fell on his knees in the trail. He wrapped his arms around the thin neck. Kävik lifted his head and licked the boy's face, and then Andy knew he was not dreaming. This was really his dog, and in some marvelous, unbelievable way he was back again.

"Kävik," Andy murmured, putting his head down against the dog's, "it's really you! It's really you! How did you get here? What happened to you, Kävik? What happened?"

Kävik could only lick his face, and continue to whine.

Andy wanted to carry the dog home, but then he saw the terrible swelling on his hip. When he tried to turn Kävik so he could lift him, the dog cried out with pain. There was no way Andy could carry him without hurting him more. For the short distance left, he would have to continue his painful way.

"Come, boy," Andy said gently. "We're going home. You can make it. Come on."

They went slowly along the trail over which they'd run pell-mell so often in the past. Andy walked close beside the dog, his hands steadying the weak animal. Kävik hobbled

*When he tried to turn Kävik so he could lift him, the dog cried out with pain.*

beside him, every step a painful, deliberate effort that took all his strength and racked his wasted body. So they made their way through the trees with many stops to rest.

Andy's mother saw them approaching from the kitchen window, and ran out. She looked at Kävik, then at Andy. "Kävik!" she said. "Kävik!"

Andy's father was coming up the trail from the cannery, and she called to him, "Kurt, it's Kävik!" Then she dropped on her knees before him and ran her hands gently down his sides and over his big head. "Oh, Kävik," she crooned, "where did you come from? What happened to you?"

"He was waiting for me back there in the trees just like he used to," Andy said. "I couldn't believe it. I'd have carried him home, but that hind leg . . . Maybe it's broken or something. I didn't dare try to lift him."

Kurt knelt beside the dog, too, and touched him with big, gentle hands. "You've had a rough time, boy! You've had a mighty rough time!"

Kävik could only stand there, balancing weakly on three legs, and wave his pitiful brush of a tail.

Laura jumped up purposefully, "Bring him on to the house right away. I'll get a blanket. He needs food. He's almost starved." She ran back into the house.

Kävik went ahead again in the same painful, jerky hop, a step and a rest, a step and a rest. Kurt was on one side of him, Andy on the other. Their hands steadied the dog, and their voices encouraged him. "You can do it," Andy's father kept saying. "Just a little more. Just a few steps."

And Kävik was doing it. His mouth was open, panting with effort, and his yellow eyes were fixed unwaveringly on the open kitchen door. He tried to hurry, but he could not.

When he hobbled through the door, Laura had a blanket spread on the floor in the corner of the kitchen where it had always been.

Kävik reached the blanket, turned around painfully once, and collapsed with an exhausted sigh. He lay full length, scarcely breathing, his eyes closed. In spite of his injury and his terribly emaciated condition, he was utterly at peace and contented at last. The terrible, driving instinct that had drawn him from two thousand miles away and had taken him across a great winter-locked mountain range, almost impassable glaciers, and river breakups was gone. He had kept faith with the greatest demand of his life. He was lying in the one spot where he wanted to be, soaking in remembered warmth and family closeness, hearing the voices he wanted to hear, and being soothed by these loving hands.

Things began to happen in rapid succession. Andy's mother was busy heating a bowl of milk. His father knelt beside the dog, and stroked him gently. He looked at the swollen hind leg, and murmured wonderingly: "I can't believe it. I can't believe it. All that way. How'd he ever do it? How'd you do it, boy?" He turned to Andy and said, "Go get Vic Walker."

"Now?" Andy asked. "He always said to come when it was dark."

"Tell him I said to get over here now!" Andy had never heard his father's voice so commanding and sharp. "Tell him it's Kävik and he's got a broken leg or something."

"But what if he won't . . ." Andy began.

"Then we'll figure some way to carry Kävik right into his office in broad daylight so the whole town can see," Kurt said angrily. "You tell him I said that."

"Yes, sir!" Andy said, and ran.

Old Mrs. Nichols was just leaving the doctor's office when Andy burst in. Dr. Walker glanced up, frowning, then asked, "Well, Andy?"

"Can you come to the house right away?" Andy panted.

"Kind of early to leave the office. Can't it wait?"

"No, sir. Dad said right away."

Dr. Walker stood up and reached for his coat and black bag. "What's the emergency?"

"Kävik's home."

Dr. Walker stopped and looked at Andy. "The dog? That wolf I doctored last winter? I thought Hunter took him south with him."

"Yes, sir. He did."

"Let's get this straight. Hunter's come back and brought the dog with him and something's happened to him? Is that what you're saying?"

"No, sir," Andy rushed on. "Mr. Hunter's still down in Washington, as far as we know. But Kävik's here. We don't know where he came from or how he got here. But he's in terrible shape. He looks half starved and he's got a broken hind leg or something. Dad says you should come right away."

Walker's black eyes began to snap. "I told you that where that dog's concerned you should come at night. Remember?"

"Yes, sir," Andy said. Then he sucked in a deep breath and threw his father's threat at Dr. Walker: "Dad says if you don't come right now, he'll carry Kävik over here to your office so the whole town can see."

Dr. Walker looked hard at Andy. "He's just bullheaded

enough to do it, too." He reached for his coat and bag. "All right," he said. "Let's go."

Walker questioned Andy as they hurried along. "Where'd you find the dog?"

"Right about here," Andy said. "He was standing in the trail waiting for me when I came home from school."

"Hunter's not here, and he didn't send him north with somebody else?"

"No, sir. Not that we know of. He's traveled an awful long way, Dad says."

"Hm-m-m," Walker mused. "Sounds interesting."

Kävik had just finished a big bowl of warm milk when they walked in. Dr. Walker bent over him, and the three people stood by anxiously. He went over the dog carefully, talking, asking questions as he worked. Finally he sat back on his heels and looked at Kävik. "Well," he said, "he's taken quite a beating in more ways than one. I'd guess he hasn't had anything to eat in about a week. He's traveled a long way. His pads are all cut and scarred, and he's got a lot of fresh scars on his body. This dog's been in a terrific fight or a couple of fights."

"Him in a fight?" Kurt said. "Not Kävik."

"Some animal has done a pretty good job of chewing him," Walker said. He unfastened the collar from around Kävik's neck and handed it to Laura. "He didn't have this on before, as I remember. It's got some mighty big teeth marks on it."

"Maybe Mr. Hunter put it on him," Andy said.

Kurt shook his head. "Mr. Hunter didn't want a collar on him. Said it'd spoil the wolf look."

"Somebody wanted one on him." Walker moved his

inspection to the injured leg again. "It's not broken," he announced after a moment. "It's been wrenched out of the socket. I'd guess it's been out quite a few days." He shook his head. "I'm surprised he traveled at all. No wonder he's nearly half starved. That wolf strain is amazingly tough. Amazing!" He opened his bag and began selecting instruments. "I'll put him to sleep and snap his hip back into the socket. Then we'll put it in a cast for four or five days, and he'll be as good as new."

"He's going to be all right?" Andy asked anxiously.

"Of course he is. He's still alive—he drank that milk. He's going to need plenty of food and rest. As for the leg, the cast will hold it in place until his muscles take over again. It'll be sore, and he'll favor the leg for a few days. But with exercise it'll strengthen. In two weeks you'll never know anything had happened to him."

In less than an hour Kävik's hip was back in place, the cast was on, and Dr. Walker was ready to leave. "Give him about five days in that cast," he said to Kurt. "Then cut it off with your jackknife. Well, that's it." He stood looking down at Kävik, who was beginning to wake up. "He's a mighty tough animal. He should have died that other time."

"Vic," Kurt asked, "do you think he walked all the way from Hunter's home? I can't believe that's possible. Why, it's over two thousand miles."

"It certainly seems impossible," Walker agreed. "But here he is. We can't argue that. And by the looks of him he hiked a lot of it. Seems he's learned something a lot of us never do."

"What's that?"

"You can do anything you have to. It'd be interesting if

he could talk. I'll bet he'd have a humdinger of a story to tell." He snapped his bag shut, prepared to leave.

"I'll bring you some money tomorrow on my way to school," Andy said.

Dr. Walker nodded. "Make it a dollar, Andy. That'll pay for the cast and the shot."

Laura shook her head, smiling. "Victor, you'll never get rich."

"If I'd wanted to, I'd have gone to Anchorage or some other city," Walker grunted. "Anyway"—he nodded at Kävik—"this was for him. He earned it fifty times over." He bent and scratched Kävik's ears. "You're quite a dog," he said. "Quite a dog."

At dinner that night Kävik managed to hobble to his feet and stand at Andy's elbow to beg tidbits as he had before. Andy and his mother both fed him.

Kurt watched them, and scowled. "You're both working yourselves up a lot of hurt," he said. "Kävik still belongs to Mr. Hunter. He'll want him back when he comes this summer."

"If we have to give him back, we have to," Laura said. "But that's no reason we can't love him while he's here. It's not Kävik's fault he doesn't want to stay with Mr. Hunter. I wouldn't either."

"I just don't see any sense letting yourselves in for more hurt," Andy's father pointed out stiffly.

"Maybe we should shoot Kävik," Laura said, showing a rare burst of temper, "or put him in a cage and shove his food in to him with a stick. Well! Andy and I aren't afraid of getting hurt." With a defiant gesture she gave Kävik a whole slab of meat, and he gobbled it down.

Kurt returned to his dinner, and said nothing.

Till now Andy hadn't thought of George C. Hunter or what his return this spring would mean to Kävik. That rock settled in his stomach again, bigger than ever.

Kävik slept on his old blanket in the kitchen that first night. Andy heard him moving about in the middle of the night, and rose to investigate. His mother joined him at the head of the stairs, and they descended together. The light was on in the kitchen. They opened the door to find Kurt bending over Kävik, pouring him a fresh bowl of milk.

Laura folded her arms and smiled archly. "Who's letting who in for more hurt?" she asked.

"He was thirsty," Kurt said sheepishly. "And he was hungry. Look at him lapping up that milk."

"You could tell that from upstairs in bed?"

"Well, he was," Andy's father defended. "You can see."

"I'm going back to bed," Laura said. "Come on, Andy."

School let out the next day. After that, Andy had two weeks' free time. Then the salmon run would begin, and most of the men in Copper City would go fishing. Andy hoped to return to work at Tom Murphy's Hardware Store for the summer.

During this free time Andy gave Kävik all his attention, and never was a dog better cared for. Kävik spent all day lying on his blanket in the kitchen, sleeping. He woke up only to eat. Each night Andy got the comb and brush out and worked on his ragged coat. Gradually it regained its wolf-gray color and sheen. Kävik was so thin that after the first few nights Andy easily carried him upstairs and put him on the rug beside the bed. In the morning he carried him down again. But Kävik gained rapidly, and his weight and strength returned. On the fifth day Andy's father cut the cast away. Kävik put his foot gingerly on the floor, and began to limp about the room. And that night he laboriously climbed the stairs himself.

Andy's father sat back on his heels, studying the dog; then he said: "Don't take him downtown, Andy. Remember what happened the other time when he ran into that pack of mongrels? The beating he took in the plane wreck caused that timidity. He's taken another beating trying to get home. Now he's probably more timid than ever. Keep him here at home."

"I will," Andy said. "But if he should get there somehow, and that Blackie or any of those others bother him, I'll take a club to 'em."

Seiners began arriving. Soon the bay at the cannery was choked with boats. When Andy went to town, the city dock was lined with boats. Booted fishermen tramped the town's one street, awaiting the opening of the season. Andy could almost feel the electric tension that gripped everyone.

Kävik had recovered marvelously, and by the time opening day arrived no one would have guessed at the ordeal he'd been through. He was again strong and vital, a big healthy animal who trotted with a spring in his step, head up, yellow eyes taking in everything. Andy could have been completely happy but for one thing. Mr. Hunter would arrive any day and see his dog. The knowledge was a black cloud over the Evans household.

Andy tried to talk to his father about it. "Maybe this time we can buy Kävik, Dad. Maybe since he ran away and all, Mr. Hunter will be willing to sell him."

"Maybe," his father said.

"Will you ask him, Dad? Will you try?"

"All right," his father agreed. "I'll try. But don't expect

anything. Mr. Hunter's a tough, stubborn man. He makes up his own mind. The fact that Kävik ran away, if he did, might make him more determined to keep him."

"Maybe he knows what a coward Kävik is now—" Andy began.

"I told him before and got nowhere," his father interrupted. "I'll try to buy Kävik, if Mr. Hunter gives me the ghost of a chance. That's the best I can promise you, Andy. Now stop plaguing me."

Andy said no more. He tried to take his mother's advice and enjoy Kävik as much as possible. But it was hard when each day some new thing happened that made him realize that Mr. Hunter would soon return.

Opening day arrived. Copper City emptied of men; the fishing fleet put to sea; and the cannery doors swung open to await the first boatload of salmon. Andy returned to work at the hardware store.

Andy's mother locked Kävik in the kitchen with her when he left for work. A half hour later she'd let him out. In the evening, before Andy was to come home, she'd call Kävik and close him in the kitchen with her until Andy arrived. In that way Kävik was kept away from Copper City and Blackie and his pack of mongrels. But every night when it was time for Andy, Kävik scratched and whined at the door.

Andy waited fearfully for Mr. Hunter.

After the first week of fishing season his father said: "Hunter probably stopped off on the way here to look at some of his other interests. He'll be along one of these days."

On Wednesday of the second week, Andy started home for the night. He was passing the Alaska Bar when Pinky

Davis hailed him through the open door. "How's it going, Andy?"

"All right," Andy said. He and Pinky were on speaking terms again, but Andy hadn't forgiven the fat little bartender for calling Kävik a rabbit.

As if in answer to the thought, Kävik entered the far end of the street and trotted happily toward Andy. Andy started to run to the dog to lead him out of sight before anyone would see him. But it was too late. Kävik broke into a run.

Pinky Davis shouted: "For Pete's sake, the rabbit's back! Hey, Andy, where'd the rabbit come from?"

Andy just stood there feeling sick.

As if it had all been arranged by some evil genius, Blackie and his pack trotted into the street from between two of the stores. The whole group of dogs stopped, surprised. They looked at Kävik. Kävik stopped and looked at them. He was suddenly tense.

Pinky Davis laughed. "You'd better get the rabbit outa here quick, Andy. Blackie or that little Rags'll murder 'im."

Andy glanced about for a club. There was nothing. With fists clenched he started toward Blackie. He opened his mouth to yell when Blackie lunged toward Kävik with a bellow. The whole scrubby pack boiled noisily at his heels. Little long-haired Rags trotted from between the stores into the street. He saw the others bearing down on the lone Kävik; letting out a yelp of delight, he took out after them.

Andy watched. He could do nothing now. At any second Kävik would turn tail and run, with the whole clamoring pack pursuing him ingloriously the full length of the street. But Kävik just stood there. His wolflike head had dropped and his yellow eyes were staring straight at the advancing

Blackie. Andy wanted to yell, "Run, Kävik, run for home!" But he couldn't.

Then Kävik charged with a blood-chilling snarl. Not away from Blackie, not racing ignobly up the street, tail tucked between his legs, but straight into the face of the pack. His great jaws were sprung wide, his teeth gleamed.

Andy had heard how wolves fought, what tremendous strength their jaws possessed, how their teeth could slash and rip with the speed of knives. Now he saw it.

Blackie was several lengths ahead of the pack. Kävik's lunge caught him squarely in the chest and hurled him rolling in the dust. Kävik was on him in a flash, driving for the unprotected throat. Blackie let out one startled bleat of surprise and fear; then Kävik's jaws snapped and ripped. Blackie never regained his feet. The pack was on Kävik then, and buried him beneath the sheer weight of their numbers.

Kävik disappeared beneath their straining bodies. The next instant he heaved into sight, rearing to his full height on hind legs in the very center of the pack, twisting, turning, teeth slashing right and left. He was leaping and dodging through the snarling dogs so fast it seemed to Andy he must be two dogs fighting at once. The scrubby pack had never met anything like this. They were used to easy victories over the softer town dogs. Their fighting howls turned to yelps and cries of pain and fright.

A rangy mongrel hobbled frantically off on three legs. A white, short-haired dog ran blindly up the street, the side of his face laid open. Then the whole pack disintegrated as dogs scattered, terrified, in all directions to escape the demon in their midst.

Little Rags, rushing in to join in the battle, skidded to a

stop. Kävik spotted him, and charged. Rags scrambled for the nearest escape, a hole under the old wooden sidewalk. Never had his short legs pumped so fast or with so great a reason. He dived headfirst into the hole, and Kävik's big jaws snapped behind his disappearing tail.

Kävik glared in at the shaking Rags. He ripped and tore at the rotting sidewalk, uttering bloodcurdling growls. Suddenly he left off and trotted to the middle of the deserted street, where he stood, head up, sharp ears pricked forward, yellow eyes looking all about. The only dog in sight was Blackie. And he was dead. Kävik's very air challenged every dog in Copper City. Here was Kävik, the wolf dog. The leader of the team that had won the North American Sled Dog Derby in Fairbanks.

Andy found his voice and called Kävik to him. He put an arm around the dog's neck and looked at Pinky Davis. He was shaking with excitement, and his voice was a little high. "Did you call him Rabbit, Pinky? You still think he's a rabbit?"

Pinky Davis looked at Kävik, at the open mouth with the rows of big white teeth, and at the yellow eyes looking steadily back at him. He glanced into the street at the dead Blackie, and sputtered, "Holy mackerel! Holy mackerel, Andy. That animal, he's a killer. He's a killer, Andy!"

"He's part wolf," Andy said. "His name's Kävik. It means wolverine."

"I believe you," Pinky Davis said. "Killed old Blackie, scattered that whole bunch. I believe you, Andy."

A voice called behind Andy, "Boy! You, boy! Come over here."

Andy turned, and there was Mr. Hunter standing across the street in front of the post office. He had a handful of

185

letters. "Boy!" he called again. "You and the dog. Come over here."

Andy said, "Come on, Kävik." He turned and ran up the street with the dog leaping beside him. Behind him, Mr. Hunter's voice shouted, "Boy! Wait up. Boy!"

Andy ran all the way home and burst into the kitchen. His mother was getting dinner, and his father was sitting at the table reading the paper.

"Dad! Mother!" he cried. "He's here. He's here! He's seen Kävik! He's coming to get him!"

Both parents looked startled. His mother said, "Who's here?"

"Mr. Hunter. He's seen Kävik. He's coming after him right now. I know he is."

Andy's father laid down the paper and asked calmly: "Mr. Hunter's here? He hasn't been to the cannery. Where'd you see him? Calm down, Andy, and begin at the beginning."

Andy drew a deep breath, and said, "When I got off work, Kävik came right into town to meet me."

"So that's where he disappeared to," his mother said. "I couldn't find him to put him in the kitchen. He must have figured out the reason."

"Did that bunch of curs get to him?" his father asked.

Andy nodded, and told them what had happened. The fight lost nothing in his telling. "Mr. Hunter was standing in front of the post office with a bunch of letters. I just know he saw it all. He yelled at me to wait. But I didn't. I know he's coming, Dad! I know it."

"He stopped to pick up the mail before going on to the cannery," Andy's father said. He looked down at Kävik then, and seemed to forget about George C. Hunter.

"So you found your courage again, after all you must have gone through," he said wonderingly. "But how?"

Andy's mother leaned down and patted Kävik's big head. "Maybe he found something to fight for. Something that was very important to him. Did you, Kävik?"

"What?" Andy's father wondered.

"Who knows?" she said, still talking to the dog. "Somebody thought enough of you to put that big collar on you. Did you love him, maybe fight for him? Or maybe you had a mate. Did you have a mate, Kävik?"

Kävik waved his tail and lifted his lips in a grin.

"If somebody loved him so much, why didn't he stay with them?" Andy's father asked. "If he had a mate, where is she?"

"We'll never know," Andy's mother said softly. "But one thing I do know. He came back to us because he loves us so much."

Andy's father continued looking at Kävik as if he were seeing him for the first time. He rubbed his big chin and shook his head.

Andy, who'd been watching out the window, cried: "Here he comes! I knew he'd follow me home. Dad, do something. Please!" Andy begged. "Try to buy him, Dad. Please, try."

As Kurt Evans walked out the door, he did not answer. Andy and his mother followed, with Kävik between them. The four of them waited in the yard for Mr. Hunter.

George Hunter stopped before Andy's father, but his eyes were on Kävik. "So he came back here. I couldn't believe it when I saw him in town just now. How'd he do it, Kurt?"

"I was hoping you could tell us," Andy's father said. "He

showed up here over three weeks ago, one hind leg out of the socket, almost starved to death. He had a lot of new scars from fighting. Somebody put a collar on him. Did you?"

George Hunter shook his head. "He ran away one night at my club. I advertised for a week, but nothing came of it. I figured he'd taken off into the hills back of the club." He frowned, black eyes staring hard at Kävik. "How'd he get here? It's more than two thousand miles. And who put a collar on him? And where'd he learn to fight? Down home he was the biggest coward I've ever seen. But not now. I just saw him kill that big black mongrel and scatter the whole mangy pack. What a sight! Standing there in the middle of the street, he looked just like he did when he won the North American. King of the world! I'm glad I found him again."

Kurt Evans said nothing. He rubbed the back of his neck thoughtfully, then his big jaw. He scowled down at Kävik, then at Mr. Hunter.

"Something wrong, Kurt?" Hunter asked.

Andy's father kept rubbing his jaw. Finally he drew a deep breath, like a swimmer about to plunge into icy water, and said, with measured deliberation, "Mr. Hunter, I can't let you take Kävik."

George Hunter's black eyes bored into Kurt Evans for a long, surprised moment. Then he said: "I bought that dog. I've got a bill of sale for him. Maybe you'd better explain, Kurt."

"I'll try. When Andy found him after the plane wreck, you told me to shoot him. Well, I didn't, as you know, and he recovered. Then you took him south. He ran away after you'd had him there for months. Somehow he got back here to us, so his running away wasn't just a spur-of-the-moment thing. He didn't want to stay with you. He wanted us because this is his home. We're his family. You had your chance with him, Mr. Hunter, and he said No. We did the right thing the first time, and gave him back to you. After all he went through to get here, what he wants this time should be considered."

George Hunter's black eyes were cold, his voice deadly, "This is the craziest thing I've ever heard. Are you just taking him, Kurt?"

"I'll buy him from you."

"I paid $2,000 for him."

Kurt Evans swallowed. "That's a lot of money."

"He was a lot of dog when I bought him. He is again."

"I've got $800," Andy said stoutly. "You can have that, Dad."

Laura, who had never taken her eyes from Kurt's face, said, "Be still, Andy."

Andy held his breath and watched his father.

Hunter said: "If you're thinking of fighting me in court, forget it, Kurt. I can beat you to death with the change in my pocket."

Kurt nodded heavily. "I know that." He was looking down at Kävik, and the yellow eyes of the dog gazed steadily back into his. "It seems to me that sometimes too much store is put in legal ownership," he said thoughtfully. "What about moral ownership, or—or a feeling of belonging somewhere special? It's not ownership with us. Kävik's part of this family. He belongs. He proved it when he came back more than two thousand miles. Now we ought to look at his side of it. This is where he wants to be. If I let you take him, without putting up some sort of fight, then I'm a traitor to him. It's like saying loyalty and devotion don't stand for much. And I don't believe that, Mr. Hunter. I know Kävik's just a dog to you, to buy and sell, or to do with as you like. It's not that way with me. I have to fight for him. I just have to fight for what I believe."

"How do you figure to do that, Kurt?" George Hunter asked caustically. "A judge or jury would laugh such a defense right out of the courtroom."

Evans continued, following his thought: "I'd guess you had some serious problems with Kävik down south. I'll bet you discovered it's a real chore to keep such a big, active dog on a city lot. So you had him confined. That's one of the reasons he ran away. And he will again if he gets the chance. You're going to have no end of trouble with this dog in the city. He belongs up here, and I think you know it. As the winner of the North American last year, he could have been worth $2,000. But there'll be a new winner this year. Half that sum would be big money for him now. I'll give you a thousand, Mr. Hunter."

"And I lose a thousand?"

Kurt Evans met George Hunter's sharp black eyes. "You won't lose a cent!" he said in a calm, sure voice.

"How so?"

"That big seiner of yours that you wanted me to take is still lying down there at the dock, doing nothing. You've tried three skippers on her in three years, and none of them have worked out. So the *Hustler* spends half the season tied to the dock, waiting for a good skipper when she should be out seining for your cannery, bringing in thousands of salmon a season. Well, I can work that boat, Mr. Hunter, as we both know. I'll take her off your hands. The same terms you offered me before. Interested?"

George Hunter's black eyes looked into Kurt Evans's calm gray ones. Evans was right about keeping such an animal on a city lot. Tearing through his wife's flower gardens once had been enough. Finding Kävik again presented too much of a problem at home. But, more important, here was a way to get Evans seining for him again. He thrust out a hand. "You've got a deal."

They shook hands, and Kurt said: "I'll go aboard the first thing in the morning and get the *Hustler* ready. You round up a crew. There's still two and a half weeks of fishing left. At the rate the salmon are running, we should have the first load in the cannery within a few hours."

"Good enough." George Hunter looked down at Kävik, then at Andy. "You've got quite a dog there, boy!" he said, and strode down the hill toward the cannery.

The Evans family returned to the house and their neglected dinner. Once again Kävik waited for tidbits at Andy's elbow.

Kurt looked at his wife, and smiled suddenly. "Seems I'm going to be a seiner again. You know, I'm glad. I should have gone back long ago."

"I know." Andy's mother smiled. "I'm happy it's over—"

Andy had pushed back his chair and was holding Kävik's head in his hands. He spoke to him in a low, intimate voice. "I wish I knew all the things that happened to you— where you've been and the people you met. How you got those scars, who put the collar on you. I'd like to know how you got your courage back again. And I'd like to know how you came back all those miles to us. But it doesn't really matter. You're home again—home for good. But I wish I knew. I just wish I knew."

Kävik cocked his head and listened to the boy's voice. Then he licked Andy's face and lifted his lips in a grin as if he understood what the words were all about.